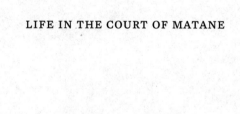

LIFE IN THE COURT OF MATANE

# Eric Dupont

# LIFE IN THE COURT OF MATANE

*Translated from the French by Peter McCambridge*

QC FICTION

Revision: Katherine Hastings, Arielle Aaronson
Proofreading: David Warriner, Riteba McCallum
Book design and ebooks: Folio infographie
Cover & logo: YQB MÉDIA
Fiction editor: Peter McCambridge

ISBN 978-1-77186-076-5pbk; 978-1-77186-077-2 epub; 978-1-77186-078-9 pdf; 978-1-77186-079-6 mobi/pocket

Legal Deposit, 3rd quarter 2016

Bibliothèque et Archives nationales du Québec
Library and Archives Canada

Published by QC Fiction
6977, rue Lacroix
Montréal, Québec H4E 2V4
Telephone: 514 808-8504
QC@QCfiction.com
www.QCfiction.com

QC Fiction is an imprint of Baraka Books

Printed and bound in Quebec

Trade Distribution & Returns
Canada and the United States
Independent Publishers Group
1-800-888-4741 (IPG1);
orders@ipgbook.com

Société de développement des entreprises culturelles

We acknowledge the support from the Société de développement des entreprises culturelles (SODEC) and the Government of Quebec tax credit for book publishing administered by SODEC.

Financé par le gouvernement du Canada | Funded by the Government of Canada | Canada We acknowledge the financial support of the Government of Canada through the National Translation Program for Book Publishing, an initiative of the Roadmap for Canada's Official Languages 2013-2018: Education, Immigration, Communities, for our translation activities.

We acknowledge the support of the Canada Council for the Arts for our publishing program.

# Contents

# Preface

I TURNED FORTY RECENTLY, the age my grandmother was when I came into the world. This made me wonder how I would react if, on a trip back in time, I happened to come across the little boy I once was. I wonder if he would agree to become my friend and, especially, if he would let me be his friend. I very much doubt it. In his eyes, I would have all the flaws his parents had—or at least those he would be able to see on the rare occasions we managed to meet, since I work all the time. He would certainly note my appalling propensity, inherited from my father, to suspect others of being as dumb as a stump. Although we might both like the same music. One thing's for sure: I'd probably get on his nerves, telling him to calm down all the time, insisting that things would work out just fine, that becoming an adult would end many of the torments of childhood. Far from being consoled, he would think I wasn't taking his troubles seriously. In short, I wonder if we would have much in common. His verbosity would annoy me, I'm sure. Plus, I don't like people who live in fear, and this boy was, if memory serves, absolutely terrorized three days out of five. He would have a very strong country accent, too. Concerned for his education, I would correct his pronunciation. He would be offended and end up hating me forever. Perhaps it's for the best that we never did meet.

I puzzled over questions like this for the longest time. In photographs from the 1970s, my feet rooted in the soil of the Gaspé Peninsula, I don't recognize my recollection of how things were. At least, I think I recognize myself, because these photos belong to me, not to someone else. What I mean is that it's only recently that I've managed to feel the slightest empathy for the little boy I used to be. Those years were long. I only know one way to describe what I felt when I understood, at age thirteen, that my childhood was over: at last. At the end of a silty childhood strewn with frustrations, silences, and things we were forced to forget, the trials and tribulations of my teenage years suddenly seemed like light entertainment.

For the longest time, I tried to understand what set me and my sister apart from other people in how we felt about our childhood. I think I have the beginnings of an answer. Very early on, long before other people, we understood that we were all alone. People will say that children live outside an adult world that tolerates them only because they are destined to grow up. Perhaps. But when I look at it like that, I think we're confusing voluntarily cutting yourself off from the adult world with the state of solitude that comes from what I will call—bluntly and for lack of a less shocking, less upsetting term—being abandoned. Sometimes we must resign ourselves to the harshness of vocabulary.

This solitude was revealed to me the day we arrived at the Thénardiers', the family that appears at the very start of this novel. When I began writing these stories, I was going to describe the Thénardiers' world. But a faithful description of all that we went through with that family would have plunged the story into a bottomless pit. My book would have foundered in the cold depths of sadness and commiseration, where the crystal-clear notes of my mother's laughter can no longer be heard. The year 1975-76 was therefore passed over. Looking back on it now, perhaps that story would have helped me reconcile myself with the child I was then. It would, at least, have explained my little earthquakes, a charming expression I owe to the American singer Tori Amos, who sang a song called "Little Earthquakes" in the early 1990s. Its tone, its words, and its severity correspond precisely to the all-too-precise memories I still have of my year with the Thénardiers. The Northern Irish have a euphemism they use whenever they speak of the war that tore their country apart: the Troubles. Each to his own avoidance strategies. I set out with the intention of going beyond euphemisms, of describing the Great

Terror, but it was another singer who convinced me to do no such thing. The wonderful Pierre Lapointe's "Pointant le nord" reminded me how important it can be not to say too much. "No, I won't speak," he keeps singing, like a mantra. I think that, to understand this novel, readers must listen to "Little Earthquakes" and "Pointant le nord." Both songs might just be the ideal preface to these stories.

Writing this novel allowed me to shut away in the basement the awful beasts that used to lay down the law in my house. Some nights, I can hear them wheezing and sighing through the floorboards. One day, out of respect for the nomadic ways my childhood taught me, I will move out of this house, perhaps even away from this city. I fully intend to leave those beasts right where they are. I don't want anyone else to see me walking them around on a leash through the streets, like children dragged along behind dogs that are too big for them. They will die of tiredness and old age, on their last legs.

My sister and I will keep on laughing like Micheline Raymond, professional cook.

"How will you convey the memories without the resentment?"

"I don't plan to."

# CHAPTER 1

# The Cat (1976)

JULY 1976. MONTREAL. The 21st Olympic Games. A tiny Romanian gymnast stands on a mat and waves to the crowd. For thirty seconds, she swings back and forth between two wooden bars, defying the laws of gravity. Her landing is perfect. She even manages a smile, and gambols away from the blue mat as though nothing out of the ordinary had happened. With the whole world looking on, she gets a perfect score. Ten. Nadia Comaneci, the child who had been getting by on an egg a day, had just revealed to Quebec's metropolis the possibilities of weightlessness. Of this impressive demonstration of grace, courage, and agility, history would remember her smile most of all—the one thing she hadn't worked on and that came to her naturally. If you walk by the Olympic Stadium in Montreal today, you'll see a monument in honour of the medal winners at the Montreal Olympics. You can't miss it. It's right by the entrance to the Biodome. Look for Nadia's name among all the others. Look up and you'll see the Romanian flag. I remember it like it were yesterday.

That summer, Radio-Canada changed its schedule so we could watch the Romanian angel fly beneath the flashbulbs. In 1976, thousands of Quebec babies were named Nadia in memory of this visit by grace personified to Montreal. Her Holiness wore a white leotard with two blue stripes down the side. On the other side of the screen, 450 kilometres east of Montreal, sprawled on an orange and yellow shag carpet, my sister and I watched Nadia perform the feats that we would later practice on our very own uneven bars: our father and mother. So, it all began with that little Romanian cat.

I've said it once, but I'll say it again: Our mother—the lower bar—loved her children, Elvis Presley, and cats (and had an impressive collection of the latter). Our father—the upper bar—loved his children, Jacques Brel, and women (and had an impressive collection of the latter). From a very young age, I knew that *Love Me Tender* and *Ne me quitte pas* were just two versions of the same song. Our mother could find intelligence in a barking dog. Our father saw stupidity in every living thing. Our mother would consult the oracles to see what the future held. Our father would regularly make a clean sweep of his life and start over. Unlike our mother, our father

16

was always itching for a fight. In our largely federalist village, he would fly the Quebec flag in front of our house. Whenever the priest visited the parish, he would wait for him, just to send him packing. He tried to grow tomatoes on the Gaspé Peninsula. In Spanish literature, he would have travelled on a donkey and battled windmills to the death. My mother conjugated verbs in the past that my father knew only in the future. My parents epitomized Quebec society in the 1970s. Sedentary yet nomadic. Yin and yang. First inseparable, then alternating with each other, these uneven bars once rent asunder by the Family Court would never meet again. My sister and I, the two children condemned to swing back and forth between them, put on an admirable display of family gymnastics for all the world to see.

In old photos from the 70s, my father looks a little like Jack Kerouac, with the indefinable charm of a man on the road. The rebel in search of a cause. He had made separatism a way of life. As far as I know, he remains the only person who managed total separation from everything. The day he no longer had children or a wife or a country to separate from, he started drinking to separate from himself. To his parents' despair, my father became the family's version of Elizabeth Taylor; or to put it more accurately, imagine a wholly convincing reincarnation of Henry VIII, King of England. Our mother, a believer faithful to the teachings of the Holy Catholic Church, was kept from the throne by various ruses and can well be imagined as Catherine of Aragon, the forlorn first wife of a king who wasn't going to be pushed around by some pope or other and who collected wives like others collect cars. Catherine of Aragon, Anne Boleyn, Jane Seymour, Anne of Cleves, Catherine Howard, and Catherine Parr filed through the king's life, with unconvincing cameos from a series of mistresses in between. And these are only some of the highlights from the remarkable skirt-chasing contest that became my father's life. My sister and I occasionally look back on the past, using these women as milestones. "Do you remember? We were still under the reign of Jane Seymour in August 1986." All the forests in Canada will never produce enough paper to adequately recount the king's love life. And even with what remains of my life, I would still run out of time before I could ever do it justice.

Our father, a police officer, was called up to protect the royal family at the Olympic Games in Montreal. My sister and I stayed in Rivière-du-Loup by the St. Lawrence with Anne Boleyn, Henry VIII's second wife. It was just after the Great Terror and just before the Great Upheaval. The Great Terror was the year of 1975–76 when my sister and I lost our grasp on the two uneven bars. For the entire year, we hurtled through the sky high above Rivière-du-Loup, with nothing to hold on to, in total free fall. That's what we were: children in free fall. We had been put in the care of a family whose name now escapes me—proof that forgetting can be a blessing—and whom we shall call, for the purpose in hand, the Thénardiers. Anyone in any doubt about what they were like need look no further than Victor Hugo. All I will say about this miserable experience with the social services is that, in the right hands, the guillotine so loved by the French can be an instrument of peace.

This is more or less what happened. When we came back from three years in Amqui, we lived by the river in an apartment in Notre-Dame-du-Portage, with a cat. Then the cat went off to hunt other mice, leaving us alone with our mother. After that, we moved into a filthy apartment with a rock-filled garden littered with old electronics equipment. Here and there lay a disembowelled television, bits and pieces of a radio, and broken glass we had to skip around while we played. Sometimes my mother stood on the rickety balcony and smoked, staring at the road, a cat at her feet. A police car raced by. Her breathing quickened as she squinted to see who was at the wheel. "Did you see if that was your father?" she asked hopefully. We couldn't tell. The road was too far away. And she would go on staring off in the direction the police car had disappeared.

One day when we found ourselves looking into an empty refrigerator, our mother brought us to the Thénardiers, whom she had found by placing an ad in the paper, and left us there while she went off to earn the money they took for looking after us. When she could no longer pay, she gave them her home, piece by piece. Almost nothing was spared: her mother's sewing machine, coats, cutlery, the dishes. We stayed there for a year until Henry VIII—on the orders of his father, who could barely contain his annoyance—came to bring us to live with him and Anne Boleyn. And that is how we wound up in a trailer in Parc de l'Amitié in Notre-Dame-du-Portage. It could have been worse, you have to admit. Why do you sigh, sister?

And so it was on the orders of another uniform that Henry VIII set off for the Olympic Games in Montreal in the summer of 1976. He would be gone for three weeks, long enough for everyone to swim, run, punch, throw, jump, shoot, pedal, and dive for all they were worth. Showing repeat broadcasts of the Olympics had forced Radio-Canada to rejig its schedule. As a result, *Heidi*, the popular Japanese cartoon, was cancelled. At the time, Canadian public television considered it more worthwhile to watch in awe as an underfed Romanian gymnast did her routine than to fret over the fate of a little cheese-stuffed Swiss girl having a nervous breakdown in Frankfurt. We felt let down by our country and could perfectly understand Henry VIII's and Anne Boleyn's desire to be rid of it as quickly as possible. Canada was clearly out of touch with its people. Sensing us lost in front of the television screen that no longer held us in its thrall, Anne Boleyn found a way to interest us in the Games. (She had no way of knowing that Quebec's revenue ministry would leave them indelibly printed on our minds: As I write this in November 2006, the government has announced that it has just finished paying off Montreal's Olympic Stadium.) Anne Boleyn told us with a laugh that the king was at the Olympics, and that we might very well see him on our colour screen. Between the hundred-metre sprints and the javelin throw, my sister and I kept an eye out for him. My money was on a running race; my sister was convinced he would be at the pool. But we were both sure we wouldn't see him anywhere near a boxing ring or a judo mat. That would have been against his nature. The king wouldn't have hurt a fly. Well, not deliberately, anyway. True to form, he would most likely have asked the fly out to dinner. He would have been charming at first. Then, as the bottles began to empty, he would have ignored her. And once he was well liquored up, he would have insulted her more and more cruelly, until she died of a broken heart with one last buzz of her wings. I have to say my father left no one indifferent. He had chutzpah in spades. Which is probably why he was sent to protect Britain's royal family at the Montreal Olympics. And of this Olympian assignment there remains one anecdote I love to tell anyone who will listen. It never fails to bring a smile to my face.

Princess Anne and her horse were taking part in the equestrian events. There's no security without the police, and back then there was no police without Henry VIII. We're talking about Quebec six years after the October Crisis, after all. It wouldn't do to find the queen's head impaled atop a fir tree in the Quebec forest. To get to the equestrian village you passed through a gate guarded by three uniformed men: a member of the Royal Canadian Mounted Police, a soldier from the

Canadian army, and a police officer from the Sûreté du Québec. Keeping guard over the equestrian village was far from exciting. All they had to do was make sure that no unauthorized visitors made their way into the part of the village reserved for the Windsors. Idle and bored, the three young men were sitting smoking on a bench, chatting about the news and generally waiting for something to happen. Suddenly, a woman with shapely thighs clad in riding breeches appeared. As she walked past, the Mountie and soldier jumped up and stood to attention, while my father sat where he was and polished off his cigarette. The lady cast an amused look at the ill-mannered police officer who continued to ogle her. He smiled at her. She went on her way. As soon as she was out of sight, the Mountie flew into a rage at him. "What the hell! Do you have any idea who that was?" My father hadn't the faintest idea who the magnificent set of thighs might belong to. "No, who was it?" he asked, crushing his cigarette stub with his shoe. "That was Princess Anne," the officer spluttered. My father smiled and said out loud what was now clear to all: the queen's daughter sure had a nice pair of thighs on her. I wonder if the princess, while stifling a yawn during another of her mother's speeches, ever casts her mind back to the ill-mannered oaf from Canada who once undressed her with his eyes like no Briton had ever dared. While Henry VIII was drooling over the generous hams of an English princess, I was busy wondering how the frail body of Nadia Comaneci could possibly withstand the repeated hammering against the uneven bars. But it's our own royal family we should be talking about here.

Catherine of Aragon. My mother. My mother's real name was actually Micheline Raymond. She was a professional cook.

Back then we lived in Rivière-du-Loup with Henry VIII and Anne Boleyn, the king's second wife. The Great Terror was behind us. We won't talk about that. We agreed to talk about something else. And I'm not really allowed to tell you about it anyway. Maman would come pick us up every Sunday to spend the day with her. We would set off in her Renault 5 for a perfect day, leaving all the recommendations of *Canada's Food Guide* far behind us. It was fries, hamburgers, spruce beer, and Gérard Lenorman all the way. I remember the song about the sad dolphin so clearly. I learned it by heart, you know. I used to sing it for my mother, who would help me out with the longer verses. Hang on a sec, I can still remember a bit of it.

*Toi, la petite Anglaise, tu rases les falaises, tu n'oses plus comme l'année dernière, me grimper sur le dos comme sur ta moto, courir après les chevaux de la mer...*

All three of us would stare at the river from the Renault 5 as we ate our fries and listened to Gérard Lenorman. So long as we were with my mother, the watery sun of eastern Quebec was almost enough to warm us up. You're never cold when you're laughing. The whales of the St. Lawrence swim up this far to give birth and feed their little ones. And every year hordes of tourists arrive from France and Germany to take in the show that my mother treated us to for free, complete with musical accompaniment.

There is a place in Rivière-du-Loup that God created just to make children happy. It's called the Point, a thin strip of land that juts out into the St. Lawrence. A narrow road runs up and down either side. The Point is on the other side of a steep hill. Where the Point begins there used to stand a small white house that served flat, round burgers barely thicker than a cookie, which meant that you had to eat two to even begin to feel full. Micheline Raymond would pull up in her car. Relish and mustard for me, relish and ketchup for my sister, and mountains—Himalayas—of fries all around. As part of a carefully choreographed Sunday ritual, she would give us the burger, which we would take in our left hand, our right hand underneath, and would proceed to eat while sitting on a picnic table, in silence, without chewing, letting it slide down our throats so as not to break apart the flesh. She would then dish out the fries in forgiveness of all past sins. These tiny hamburgers have since been replaced by other, bigger ones, each containing half a cow. Then we would drive the Renault 5 toward the broad, green river. The road hugged a rocky headland, which in one particular spot looked vaguely like the head of an Indian chief. Feathers and war paint had been daubed onto the rock in bright colours so that it was clear for all to see that it was indeed the head of an Indian looking out over the vast St. Lawrence River.

The head commanded respect, fear, and admiration. But the rock had been given its name on the most arbitrary of principles. I drove past it last summer and thought it would only have taken a different lick of paint for it to be called "The Bunch of Grapes" or "The Locomotive." At the end of the Point, the Saint-Siméon ferry berthed at a long wharf. From the mouth of this white beast cars would pour forth from elsewhere, from the water, from the sea, from somewhere on the North Shore. On the other side of the Point, the north side, we discovered a huge cardboard castle, complete with towers, right out of the Middle Ages.

After a day at the Point, my mother would drive us back to the trailer park and the court of Henry VIII. It was known as Parc de l'Amitié—Friendship Park, if you will. It was a collection of sheet-metal homes a little like railway cars, carefully positioned around a grass circle, that could each be towed off someplace else like gypsy caravans. This travelling housing development was alive with children who waged occasional bloody war on each other. The neighbouring forest served as a terrifying torture chamber. Sometimes we would spot hippie children roaming butt naked from trailer to trailer, helping themselves to the fruit baskets of the people living there, who observed the marauders in stunned silence. On weekends, evangelizing Mormons sometimes ventured into these poorer areas to spread the good news. The Mormons—men more beautiful than any of us had ever seen—came from the United States and looked like the male models in the Sears catalogue. The parting in their hair, the black suit and tie, the American accent when they spoke French—they looked like gods descending upon our miserable abodes. I was six when two Mormons came into the trailer looking to convert Anne Boleyn. They failed. I would have let them convert me in a heartbeat: they were so handsome. Now when I see them walking in pairs in the Montreal metro with their Church of Jesus Christ of Latter-Day Saints badges, I like to imagine myself as a Mormon, obsessed by genealogy, a father to nine little Mormons, playing Biblical Scrabble with the family every Tuesday evening and drinking only verbena and camomile tea.

In winter, the wind would crack the metal of our tiny homes. These lived-in containers are still scattered all across Quebec today, a sign of my country's poverty and fragility. They're built on wood blocks rather than concrete foundations, to make them easier to move. Living in one of these homes means enduring the whims of the wind. It makes you humble, banning all thoughts of vanity and pretension. Henry VIII and Anne Boleyn's house was glacial, ugly, fleeting, and rectangular. All kinds of people lived in these trailers, brought together by a love of sheet metal. A huge Russian woman, the mother of two obese children, lived in one. No one knew where her husband was hiding. Dead or alive? A spy in the pay of the USSR? No one ever saw him. We will never know what brought a Russian woman to Friendship Park at the height of the Cold War. Cries would often emanate from that trailer, terrible shouting matches. One day, the Russian woman's daughter barricaded herself in the bathroom in a fit of anger, slamming the door behind her and smashing an enormous mirror to smithereens. At Friendship Park there was no hiding your feelings from anyone. A teenager who lived two or three trailers down used to terrorize the place. She was called Diane and had been very aptly named indeed. You wouldn't have wanted to catch her by surprise, out hunting in the forest. A gaggle of other kids—these ones normal enough—lived just beside us. Further away, toward the shoreline, lived strange people who bared all in the strangest places.

Bank clerks, teachers, workmen, policemen, store-keepers, the unemployed, and welfare bums lived side by side in neatly arranged rows. Their houses were all exactly the same size, flanked by small square yards with wooden tables. Flowers in front of the trailer were the only tolerated variation. Some opted for roses, others for pansies, French marigolds, or dahlias. A field in the midst of the circle of trailers was used for ball games, baseball, and softball. Irony would have it that a Russian lady had left communism to come live in a commune worthy of Eastern Europe.

Right at the end of the row of trailers, we knew a family of separatists. We recognized their allegiance by the fact that in every conversation they gave the impression that the person they were talking to was a halfwit, while they basked in the light of Truth. One day they left and were never heard from again. Living in Friendship Park had one big benefit: the hope of leaving it someday. Because everyone left the trailer park one day. People were just passing through. When the worst came to the worst, people added extensions to their trailers to give themselves a little more room. Others put up sheds. But no matter how hard they tried, a trailer is still a trailer. People hated them while claiming to love them because you weren't supposed to hate anything or anyone at Friendship Park. Except for Nancy.

Nancy was a perfectly lovely six-year-old girl with blonde, curly hair, always in good spirits, always cheerful, and generally as nice as can be. I think, looking back now, that was precisely why we hated her. She lived alone with her parents. But one of the children had decided to despise her. I can't remember who. That was just the way it was. As soon as she showed up, we would shove her and insult her for the fun of it, telling ourselves, "If I torment her, the others will like me." We were all capable of it. At Friendship Park, just like anywhere else in the world, finding the right outlet for your hatred was vital.

In September 1976, we were all sent to school in Notre-Dame-du-Portage. Every morning we waited for a yellow school bus we could see coming from miles away, always at the same time. We would all stand in the grass circle and wait for it. Little Nancy often arrived at the last minute. She had always forgotten something. Her mitts, her hat, her catechism book. In a panic, she would ask us if she had time to go back and get whatever she had forgotten. The less cruel children advised caution. Others, eager to see her suffer, lied and told her she had plenty of time and that the bus would wait for her, when we could already see it coming in the distance. The poor girl believed them, hesitated just long enough to increase the risk factor, and foolishly returned home. Four times out of five, the bus came as she was rummaging through her trailer looking for a mitten, book, or scarf. Some of the nastier kids said she was looking for her brain. From our seats on the bus, we watched her emerge from her trailer. She broke into a run—which always raised a laugh—then the bus set off again, leaving the little blonde girl behind, arms outstretched, shouting "Wait for me!" as we smiled at her, feeling not the least bit ashamed of ourselves. As far as we were concerned, she deserved everything that came to her. Once, someone, a boy, if I remember right, expressed pity for her. We looked at him like he was from another planet. I don't know what ever became of Nancy. She's surely running to catch a bus, train, or plane somewhere.

When we came home from Sundays with my mother, the prisoners were exchanged quickly. Nothing else was exchanged. Not a look, not a word, not a sign. My mother stayed in her car, my father in his trailer. We would have to spin a few times on the lower uneven bar to build up the speed and momentum we needed to reach the upper bar. The twenty steps separating the car from the door served as a buffer between the two bars.

Readers who would like to try it for themselves at home must first understand that you need to build up enough speed and grab the bar with both hands so as not to fall flat on your face on the blue mat, which happened often enough all the same. You have to grab the upper bar as you fall back. Forget about the lower bar so you don't miss the upper bar. And above all else, never mention the lower bar. Forget all about it until the following Sunday. In Henry VIII's home, heated to 17 degrees, all the pure light from my mother's face slipped away. In the presence of the king, thoughts would turn to plots, the court, and decorum.

After one such Sunday, I once dared, in the home of the king, to utter my mother's name before Anne Boleyn. I don't know what came over me, at six years of age, to speak of such unseemly matters. I knew I should mention her only when strictly necessary. I must have been nuts to say my mother's name out loud. It was sheer provocation. Fortunately, Anne Boleyn was on the ball! Censure was sharp and swift, delivered in a rasping voice just one degree above absolute zero. "I never want to hear another word about your mother again. She abandoned you. Don't ever talk to me about her again." It was at that precise moment, I remember, that I understood the touching precariousness of those who have been given the benefit of the doubt. The start of Anne Boleyn's reign had brought the Great Terror to an end. God bless her. But as soon as she tried to wipe my mother's name from my memory, doubt set in. I also remember that, one day, in order to get into her good graces, my sister dared to call Anne Boleyn "Maman" and that the outcry had been even more vociferous. What's wrong with you, you little nitwit? What do you still need a mother for at your age? You're seven years old! Kittens are weaned at seven weeks. They don't care where they come from. And so "Maman" became a hammer word, one that made a lot of noise and drew disapproving looks. They are practical because you can use them to drive nails home or pull them out, but they should be used sparingly.

From that moment on, I took pity on Anne Boleyn for thinking that she could win, that things were going to turn out differently for her. I took pity on her because everyone aspires to be No. 1, but she could only be No. 2. Think about it: if Nadia Comaneci had won the silver medal in Montreal, would anyone remember her name? Do you really think so? So go on then, who came in second on the uneven bars in Montreal in 1976? Not so easy, is it? Her name was Teodora Ungureanu. She wasn't a bad gymnast, far from it. She was way better than you or me. Her only flaw was that she wasn't Nadia Comaneci. That she wasn't No. 1. There you go. Quebec's registry offices have recorded precious few Teodoras. And I guarantee that most Nadias in Quebec who are turning thirty this year are secretly thanking the Romanian champion for giving her all. That's the problem in a nutshell. Everyone wants to be a Nadia. No one wants to be a Teodora. Anne Boleyn never stood a chance. The day when, after stripping Catherine of Aragon of her royal titles, King Henry VIII had Anne Boleyn crowned, the new queen got a hostile reception as she passed by. Out on her decorated barge on the Thames, Anne Boleyn couldn't make Londoners forget that the real queen was still alive. She was booed by the people, who preferred Catherine, a devout Catholic. For the rest of her reign, Anne Boleyn was despised; first by the people, for whom she was nothing more than a crown grabber, then by the court because she had too much influence on the king, and finally by the king himself, who wound up having her executed. Hence the importance of never being No. 2 and always eating your hamburger with your eyes closed.

Little Nadia wasn't the only one making the news back then. In 1975, somewhere in England, a certain Margaret Thatcher had been elected leader of the Conservative Party. Britain's education minister from 1970 to 1974 had made a name for herself by putting an end to free school milk, earning her the unflattering nickname Margaret Thatcher, Milk Snatcher. But she didn't stop there. She was elected Britain's prime minister in 1979, transforming England by giving the country its productivity back. For Mrs. Thatcher, self-satisfaction could only come about by putting all thoughts of laziness to the back of one's mind. A hard woman, she was blind to the social dramas her austere policies caused and didn't think twice about criticizing public opinion, declaring war on Argentina, breaking the unions, or imposing unfair taxes—in short, the Iron Lady earned her nickname. "If you want something said, ask a man," she remarked. "If you want something done, ask a woman." London's Saucy Seventies—a golden age when rock singers still choked on their own vomit—gave way to Thatcher's implacable England.

I had never heard of Margaret Thatcher when I lived in Friendship Park. It was only when reading her biography years later that I had the impression of bumping into an old acquaintance. Under Anne Boleyn, trains ran on time. Life in the court was as regular as clockwork. Two and two always made four. The roars of laughter and the sheer madness that had marked the reign of Catherine of Aragon were now in the past. The time had come for education and reason. It was a new age in which women were worth more than men, mothers were interchangeable, and anything was possible as long as you applied the right mathematical formula. We had quickly learned that poetry, hugs, and kisses would get us nowhere in a court where knowledge, science, and cleanliness would be rewarded. Thanks to Anne Boleyn and her books, I foresaw the chance to walk toward the future a new man. Memories would be of no use to me. They compromised my relations with the crown. Before the monarchs, it was simply a matter of feigning approval of all their dreams and projects, all the while imagining their disappearance behind their backs and the day Henry VIII would come to his senses. I waited and learned. My every progress was noted.

Unlike Catherine of Aragon, Anne Boleyn believed that a meritocracy could distract from the gentle chains of filial attachment. In the face of family relationships that stubbornly perpetuated ignorance and mediocrity, Anne Boleyn put forward a new model free from all sentimentality, by which everyone could use knowledge to save their own skin.

It was in this spirit of discovery that I was sent to school in Notre-Dame-du-Portage in the fall of 1976. The first day, Henry VIII or Anne Boleyn (I can't remember which) came with me and talked for a long time with a little round woman with short black hair who wore a small cross and was going to take care of me. I think they talked about Catherine of Aragon, the Thénardiers, and my big sister. Sister Jeannette Jalbert strived to deliver children from their inner prisons by teaching them to read. Strangely enough, literature speaks very seldom of the women—because they usually are women—who give birth to us for a second time. In the world's great squares, there are no statues in honour of these armies of teachers who, every September, recreate the miracle of Pentecost all around the world. No chain of mountains has been named after the schoolmistresses who lay the sword of knowledge on the shoulders of millions of snot-nosed kids each year and say, "Here is the world. Do with it what you will." Sister Jeannette Jalbert, a teacher in Notre-Dame-du-Portage, Canada, would free me from the shadows of illiteracy. She started by giving us little illustrated books, with no more than a sentence on each page. It was, all in all, simple enough. Someone had drawn on the pages, and the drawings were called letters. These letters, grouped together in a certain way, had a given meaning. This meaning was called a word. By putting *a, i, g, h, h, n, r, s,* and *t* in the right order, you got "thrashing." It was simple enough. The words could then be put together to form sentences like this one: "You have to hide. Madame Thénardier is looking for you." The system could also be used to ask questions like: "Does it still hurt?" There were infinite possibilities: "Here you go, child. Now you can write what once was, what is, and what you wish there to be." This was Sister Jeannette's message in a nutshell. I drank in her words like a precious alcohol. I remember the first time I managed to decode a word, I heard something like the long whistle of a rocket taking off. Something had built up a head of steam. I moved on to decoding sentences in no time at all.

To track the progress of the twenty illiterates she was in charge of, Sister Jeannette had put a chart up on the wall, where our first and last names appeared in a vertical list. There were fourteen reading levels. The goal was obviously to reach the fourteenth level as quickly as possible. Every week she would have one of us stand up and read beside her desk. If she was happy with our reading, she would give us a little star, which we stuck beside our names. The first stars were blue, the next were red. The second-to-last stars were silver, and the very last ones were gold. Gold like Nadia. This gave me an idea of the speed at which I and the rest of my classmates were progressing. After a few weeks, head held high, I was the first to proudly stick a gold star in the very last box. Far behind, other children were still struggling to earn two or three stars. With scant regard for humility or subtlety, I bragged about my success to the others, expecting them to shower me with praise and idolize me. My hopes were dashed. One day after recess, I was admiring the glorious chart when I realized that someone had clumsily taken three of my stars and stuck them beside their own name, no doubt believing that this lamentable larceny would paper over their reading problems. I filed a complaint with Sister Jeannette. Following an investigation that lasted all of seventeen seconds, the guilty party owned up to her misdemeanour. With everyone watching, she was forced to put the tiny stars back in their rightful place. I derived no satisfaction from this exercise, which had been humiliating for all concerned. It wasn't like other cases of theft when another child stole your teddy bear, candy, or lunch. Truth be told, the star thief had taken nothing from me—to do that, she would have had to make me forget everything I had learned. And you can't force someone to forget. You could burn all the star stickers in the world in a great big pile, but nothing would ever erase what they represent. Everything you know, I told myself, will stay with you forever. All you have to do is remember it from time to time. And to do that, you need to know how to read. If you write "My mother's name is Micheline Raymond. She is a professional cook." on a scrap of paper, a rock, or a plank of wood, you're not likely to forget. Provided you don't lose the piece of paper, provided the plank doesn't go up in smoke, provided you don't forget where you put the rock, you'll remember it forever.

Being able to read put me in Anne Boleyn's good graces, which gave me access to her collection of comic books. On the other hand, despite my keen interest in reading, my dealings with Sister Jeannette were somewhat distant. The nun's apparent coolness toward me probably had something to do with the pencil incident. One day, you see, one of the illiterates stole my pencil. Just like that, right under my nose. He walked off with the pencil, without so much as looking at me. There was nothing special about the pencil. Its only quality was that it belonged to me. It was a crime against my property. I stood up, paying no heed to the fact that Sister Jeannette was in the middle of teaching us a song about Jesus. The tune was straightforward enough: "The Lord is my shepherd, Alleluuuuuuuuuia!" Sister Jeannette was first and foremost a nun. Nuns are always talking about Jesus. Jesus is the son of God and our shepherd and all that. That's the way it is. This wasn't going to get me my pencil back, and I wasn't going to wait for kingdom come to get it back either. So I got up and reclaimed my pencil, punching the crook so hard in the chest that he fell back on his ass. There then ensued a fight to the death accompanied by the cries of seals lost on the pack ice. Sister Jeannette cut her hymn short and, just as I was about to strangle the little louse, grabbed me by the hand and lifted me up off the ground, dragging me out of the classroom to the stairs. The stairs of the elementary school in Notre-Dame-du-Portage, if stairs could talk, would still have plenty to say about the scene they witnessed that day. She held me by the shoulders with the grip of a lumberjack. I yelled that she was crazy, which only made her laugh. I tried to hit her, which made her laugh even harder. I told her in an icy tone that I didn't like her, then promptly burst into tears. Tears tend to calm a nun down. We stayed there for five minutes on the stairs, me resting my head on her bosom, until I opened my eyes and saw her cross right up against my nose. I asked her why she was wearing a cross, when neither I, the king, my sister, nor Anne Boleyn had one. "Everyone has one," she replied. "You do, too." The incident was closed. The pencil thief trembled every time I walked past until June.

Classes got underway again. A few days later, Sister Jeannette sped up the rhythm of my existence even more. A huge grey book lay on a lectern. Its pages were so thin and fragile that Sister Jeannette wouldn't let us touch them. We were allowed only to look. Approaching the book was not without risk. One morning, she got us all to be quiet and asked me to come stand beside her at the lectern. Slowly she turned the book's pages, squinting and pointing to the passage I was to read out loud. The text was numbered and set out in narrow columns to make it easier to read. The pages had no pictures and had turned slightly yellow. My classmates looked at me and sniggered. A girl wriggled on her chair like she had worms. I didn't know what tone I should adopt. The occasion made me plump for solemnity and seriousness, which intimidated me a little. Sister Jeannette had often read aloud from the huge book, but she had never let one of us do it before. She told me to ignore the numbers scattered around the text. I took a deep breath and launched into the passage she had pointed to.

*Blessed are the poor in spirit: for theirs is the kingdom of heaven.*
*Blessed are they that mourn: for they shall be comforted.*
*Blessed are the meek: for they shall inherit the earth.*
*Blessed are they which do hunger and thirst after righteousness: for they shall be filled.*
*Blessed are the merciful: for they shall obtain mercy.*
*Blessed are the pure in heart: for they shall see God.*

The other children applauded. In the corner, a knucklehead studiously picked his nose. Sister Jeannette smiled. A fog of happiness enveloped the classroom. I hadn't really understood what I had read. I didn't know what "meek" or "merciful" meant. I had never met anyone like that. You have to admit it didn't take much to bring about the conversion that morning in 1976: a nun, a bible, a ban, Madame Thénardier, a promised inheritance, and a view of the St. Lawrence thrown in for good measure. Anyone can afford that.

I remembered that my mother would sometimes mention God. One day, she had brought me to a huge, freezing-cold house beside the hospital, where only women who looked like Sister Jeannette lived. The convent. She took painting classes with one of the nuns there, and I had to wait for her. She painted flowers, landscapes, vases. Her teacher spent her time smiling at me and trying to get me to say something. I didn't like it there. The convent was just up from the Thénardiers' house, at the top of the town of Rivière-du-Loup. Having the Thénardiers so close threw me into a panic. At the tender age of six, I was already looking to get as far away from them as I could. I waited impatiently for the class to end. In the convent there was a Sacred Heart below a floating paper banner that said, "I am waiting for you in the Kingdom of Heaven." Jesus was addressing the persecuted and the poor in spirit. After my triumphant reading, someone had asked Sister Jeannette what "poor in spirit" meant. She said it was when someone wasn't planning on doing wrong, when someone didn't yet know that there are things you can do and things you can't. In a split second, I wondered who among us was poor in spirit. I still don't know to this day.

I told the court of Henry VIII all about my brush with the "poor in spirit." I was as high as a kite. As far as I was concerned, Sister Jeannette had delivered the Truth to me bound hand and foot, and this Truth had come from my mouth. Anne Boleyn and Henry VIII didn't deem the matter worthy of interest. They seemed aware of the existence of the poor in spirit, without caring to wonder where they lurked among us. The king raised his eyes to heaven and said, "Typical nun!" My story was met with a touch of disdain. They stopped just short of calling me a halfwit. The kingdom of Henry VIII was not the Kingdom of Heaven. The king even had the strange habit, when he hit his thumb with a hammer, of crying "Damned nuns!" He said it when he stubbed his toe against a piece of furniture in the morning, when the electricity bill arrived, when there was no beer left, when a pot boiled over, and when his car wouldn't start in the winter.

Life at the palace continued. I now had access to all of Anne Boleyn's books. She had novels and comics. I got Tintin's *Shooting Star* for my birthday. The back cover showed all the other Tintin books. "You could collect them. One every year." At that rate it would take me twenty years to collect them all. An eternity. Fortunately, I also got one at Christmas and at the end of the school year.

The idea of collecting them summed up Anne Boleyn's nature perfectly. Accumulating little by little. Like an ant. Gaining a hold over the everyday items that would otherwise only end up at the dump. "Look after your nickels and dimes, and your dollars will take care of themselves." Common-sense accounting. Anne Boleyn may have shown a little more determination than Catherine Parr (the sixth wife), but definitely less assurance than Catherine Howard (the fifth). She ended

41

up setting me a challenge I could rise to: forgetting. The memory of my mother—as solid and implacable as Michelangelo's Pietà—towered over my father and her. The constraints of daily life with Anne Boleyn and Henry VIII prevented me from publicly defying this order to forget. The consequences would have been unfortunate. Rather than act as a third uneven bar between my mother and father—which would have helped with my movement—Anne Boleyn was the blue mat where gymnasts distracted by a flashbulb or a shout from the crowd missed the lower bar by a millimetre and fell flat on their faces. But I had watched Nadia Comaneci closely. I wouldn't miss a beat.

After the summer solstice of 1977, the wind changed at Friendship Park. My sister and I began to foresee the signs of imminent catastrophe. First, our neighbour, a kind soul and father to a number of children, started to jokingly call us the Mataners. We didn't know what a Mataner was. I presumed it was grown-up talk for rascal. Then there was a long car ride along an endless road. In an unknown town, the king and queen looked for a plot of land. We slept in awful motels. It was in this town, I remember, that Anne Boleyn found out she was pregnant. We were told in the car. Back in Rivière-du-Loup, things moved fast. Objects disappeared into boxes. People came to bid farewell to the king and queen. All to the heady scent of apocalypse. There were probably a few scarcely perceptible earthquakes. The day of the Great Upheaval, Heidi had just returned to Switzerland to learn that Peter's grandmother had died, and I think after that we reread *Hansel and Gretel*, a prophetic tale. Along with the gospel according to Matthew, Grimm's fairy tale had been my favourite literary illustration of the ways of the world. Although I found the German fairy tale more realistic. At one point, the father and wicked stepmother abandon Hansel and Gretel in the forest. Some children switch off at this point, thinking it unrealistic, that no one would ever do such a thing. Others, traumatized, put the book down altogether. I found it all completely run-of-the-mill and unoriginal. There was nothing very surprising about the whole thing if you asked me. I enjoyed the story's vivid realism.

The horror didn't end there. We would be moving to Matane, we were told, three hundred kilometres east of Rivière-du-Loup. A dizzying distance for a child of seven. They seemed pleased by the news. The king had been transferred there. At his own request. A truck came to the trailer park, and our home was lifted up off the ground and put on a platform with wheels. It followed us all the way to Matane. It reminded me of a Russian fairy tale in which a house with chicken legs spins around and around. We got in the car and set off for Matane along Route 132, our home following far behind.

As the car sped east, I took up the position that every son adopts one day or another in relation to his father. He was driving, facing forward, barely aware of the drama unfolding less than a metre away. Kneeling on the back seat, I was facing the other way, looking back as though at a plane wreck, staring open-mouthed at the crater of devastation we were leaving behind. Like Amqui before it, Rivière-du-Loup grew smaller and smaller until I could no longer see it. I was told to turn around, sit up straight, and stop surveying the wasteland behind us. Looking back could be dangerous, they said. It would make me feel sick. So I faced the other way. The licence plate on the car in front had Quebec's motto on it: "Je me souviens."

One day a chubby, loud-mouthed girl from Ontario who turned up her nose at everything that wasn't English grilled me about Quebec's motto. "What does it mean, *Dje me souvienne*?" she asked, before tucking into a fried bacon sandwich smothered in butter. I found the question idiotic. "My mother," I told her. "I remember my mother." She must have thought that Quebec had come up with a pretty humdrum motto. Everyone remembers their mother. But do they really have to go around writing it on all the licence plates? Yes, in some cases they do.

I thought I could see, running behind our car along the asphalt of Route 132, Sister Jeannette with a bible under one arm; my mother, her arms raised to the heavens in a panic; and even little Nancy, late as usual, who had missed the bus again because she had left her catechism book at home. Thrown back against the seat as the car sped forward, I heard a long whistling sound as we left Rivière-du-Loup. A new acceleration.

44

Even today, every time I drive along Route 132 east of Rivière-du-Loup, I fall into a kind of trance. Something about it upsets me. Despite the picture-postcard scenery, despite the lovely people and the smell of the sea, something presses down on my lungs, reminding me that I'm moving away from where I belong. I watch in the rear-view mirror as Rivière-du-Loup slowly recedes into the distance. It's usually at times like this that I feel my little earthquakes.

At Sainte-Flavie, they told us we had arrived in Gaspésie. The invisible line separating the Lower Saint Lawrence and the Gaspé Peninsula is much more than an arbitrary border drawn up by geographers with nothing better to do. People live quite differently to the east and west of the dividing line: The people of the Lower Saint Lawrence expect things will pick up, while those on the Gaspé Peninsula know they'll only get worse. Both sides are sometimes disappointed. When Henry VIII and Anne Boleyn told us with a smile that we had just entered the Gaspé Peninsula and the north shore of the St. Lawrence was nothing more than a thin strip of blue land, I became a Gaspé man once and for all.

At the end of that day, I stood before Matane like Attila before Rome. Looking toward the town, I wished it would just disappear. When I awoke after my first night there, I waited in vain for the TV people to come pack up the miserable set. Truth be told, the main problem with Matane was that it wasn't Rivière-du-Loup. Ironically enough, my father seemed to like Matane for the very same reason. And yet of all Quebecers, the good people of Matane are probably among the friendliest of the lot. Their cheeks have turned rosy from the wind that blows over the town three hundred and sixty-two days of the year. There, the supports below our trailer drew back, and on a cliff overlooking the sea the house fell down in a puff of smoke. We didn't stay there very long. A year or two, I think. I was seven when we moved to Matane. I had already had six addresses. In the decade I was to spend in my new town, I would have six others. Henry VIII wasn't the type to sit still. In Matane the rules of censorship were repeated even more firmly than the first time. We were given a helpful list of ins and outs:

In:     Quebec (and all its symbols)
        Anne Boleyn
        Jacques Brel
        Cod in all its forms
Out:    Canada (and all its symbols)
        Catherine of Aragon
        Elvis Presley
        Drives in the Renault 5

They couldn't have been clearer with us. In the same tone used to shout "Die, you pig, I'm gonna come spit on your grave!" the new rules of memory were presented to us. Over the years, a series of inexorable royal edicts were added. Edict 101: It is strictly forbidden to pronounce the name of Micheline Raymond, professional

46

cook. Edict 102: The eating of Cadbury products is forbidden. Edict 103: The telephone is not a toy. It is strictly prohibited to call anyone without permission. All conversations shall be supervised by the queen. Get used to it. Edict 104: The word of the Lord is outlawed in the royal court. The king and queen shall hear no talk of catechisms, nuns, the new or old testaments, or resurrection. The dead shall not rise again. Edict 105: It is forbidden to make any allusions to the past in front of the soon-to-be-born little brother. He will have to work out how we got here by himself. Edict 106: You shall lend your unfailing support to the sovereignty movement, on pain of being disowned. The fleur-de-lys is your emblem, and Quebec is your country. Edict 107: This home is no place for halfwits. It is therefore forbidden to watch television for more than one hour per day. All programs must be approved by the queen. All TVA programs are outlawed. Since we will have no truck with cable, you shall have to make do with Radio-Québec and Radio-Canada. You will thank us later. Edict 108: You shall do the dishes thrice daily, after each meal. Even when visiting. The queen shall inspect the plates. Edict 109: Saturdays are devoted to cleaning. The girl shall scour the palace bathrooms, and the boy shall ensure the floors are spotless. Everyone shall do his or her bit in the kingdom of Anne Boleyn. And even then, the queen shall not let you out of her sight as you go about your work. Edict 110: You shall respect and obey your queen, whom you shall address by her first name.

The queen's jurisdiction extends to justice, stewardship of the palace, financial management, culture, and tele-communications. You no longer have a mother. The king shall from time to time take it upon himself to remind you where you come from. For all questions about the matter, see Edict 101.

Oppression breeds revolution. The crushers will be crushed. Or at least that's what we like to believe. Anne Boleyn was a boycotter. Her strategy was a means of sur-vival. She forbade. Castrated. First came the boycott of our mother. There then followed a series of lesser bans that made everyday life tough. One of them involved Cadbury, the chocolate makers. In 1976, after the Parti québécois had been elected in Quebec, a number of English companies had seized the occasion to move their head offices to Toronto, preferring the comfort of bore-dom to the tribulations of Quebec politics. Outraged separatists launched a boycott of Cadbury (and Sun Life Insurance, among others). Chanting "Let's bar Cadbury" as their slogan, they waged war against the English manu-facturer of the sweet candy. Their movement would have left me completely indifferent at the age of seven had Anne Boleyn and the king not decided to buy into it. It was thereafter forbidden to purchase or consume any Cadbury products in the presence of the king or Anne Boleyn. The same glacial tones reserved for my mother were used to proclaim the banning of Cadbury.

There was just one problem: Cadbury was—and still is—the maker of the Caramilk bar, a chocolate bar with a soft caramel centre that at the time was high on my list of favourite things to eat. My mother would pass them to me in her Renault 5 as I sang Gérard Lenorman to her. "Caramilk" had become a hammer word. Whenever I managed to scrape together thirty cents, I would slip off to a store where no one knew me to buy a Caramilk. I had to bike for kilometres to make sure word didn't get out. Anything not to get caught. Once we were in the depths of the countryside, beyond the village of Saint-Ulric near Matane, I settled on an old general store run by two senile biddies. It belonged to a different era, an old-fashioned general store that smelled of before the war. In the deserted store, you had to wait for one of the old witches to limp her way out of the storeroom. Children in the village used to say that they had both been dead for years and we were being served by ghosts. Their memory was so shaky that I could walk into the store four times in the same day without them remembering a thing about my earlier visits. Alzheimer's guaranteed my anonymity. Even under the harshest interrogation, at best they would have been able to confirm I had been to the store. They would never have been able to betray the nature of my purchases.

The first time I did it, I remember I was wracked by guilt and high on the sweet smell of dissidence. I stood before one of the two old crones and asked for a Caramilk bar. A few seconds went by in silence. A clock struck three. Slowly, she asked me to repeat my order, tapping away at a small device lodged in her ear. "A

Caramilk! I want a Caramilk!" I repeated, pointing at the coveted candy. She turned around. I heard her bones protest. Three short steps toward a counter in disarray. From there, she looked at me to make sure she had understood, pointing to a bottle of bleach. Patience was paramount. My finger tried to guide her shaking hand toward the Caramilk. Sometimes, she would break off to ask me if I was Armand's son, a man who had probably been dead and buried for over seventy years. Then, a glimmer of reason flashed across her eyes, and her hand at last grasped the Caramilk. Her memory had also forgotten inflation. Thinking she was still in 1970, she asked me for twenty cents. Not that I was going to contradict her. I fled so that she wouldn't have to denounce me if ever the king raided the store. Then I went to the beach, the place of all outlawed activities, where Anne Boleyn never set foot because it was too windy. Hiding behind a rock, I devoured my Caramilk while looking out to sea. I had to be careful not to leave the orange and brown wrapper at the bottom of my pocket. It would have been giving myself away too cheaply. I dug a hole half a metre wide and buried it there. Today I sometimes still buy a Caramilk, eat it in secret, and burn the wrapper to destroy the evidence. I am the only Montrealer for whom eating a Caramilk is a subversive, revolutionary act.

Back home, some first-rate lying covered my tracks. Always have an alibi. In the court of Anne Boleyn and Henry VIII, the sovereignty-association debate had plumbed the depths of the most commonplace candies. Some of their most memorable mini-boycotts included religious education, the TVA television network, my sister wearing makeup, anything made by non-unionized workers, and visits to relatives Anne Boleyn didn't like. Boycotts invariably lead to other boycotts, until everybody ends up boycotting everything. After boycotting the Moscow Olympic Games in 1980, the tables were turned on the Americans when the Soviets boycotted the Los Angeles Games in 1984. What goes up must come down, apart from Cadbury, that is. Since 1976, the company has more than doubled in size, in spite of the separatist boycott. It just goes to show that sugar always wins in the end.

It was at this same time that, almost everywhere in Quebec, the *hood du char* started to be called the *capot de la voiture* and it became frowned upon to *canceller* one's appointment. If you wanted to *annuler* it, that was fine. *Hamburgers* became *hambourgeois*, and *hotdogs*, *chiens chauds*. At the peak of this pile of grotesque terminology decrees sat the innocent T-shirt, henceforth a *gaminet*. The idea was to make a clean break from the past in all its forms. New words for a new world. The words *father* and *mother*, which had until then always occupied a clearly defined semantic field, were now elastic terms. One was just as good as the other; the roles had become interchangeable. We belonged to a new gender, a new race of humans that wouldn't trouble itself with the morals of another age. Once independent, we would be like androgynous gods. We had painted a huge fleur-de-lys in royal blue on the wall of one of the homes we lived in. Our sovereigns dreamed of sovereignty. One man's name cropped up more and more frequently in conversation. Far from being a hammer word, his name brought a sparkle to the eyes of the king and queen: René Lévesque.

"Who's that?"

"René Lévesque."

"What's he doing?"

"He's leading us to independence."

So sovereignty was a place you needed a guide to get to. A little like Matane. A man brings you there for your own good. Only René Lévesque had decided to ask the people before throwing the house on the back of a truck. While our questions about sovereignty were sometimes answered in great detail, any inquiries about the relationship between Anne Boleyn and us met with varying reactions, depending on whether we asked the king or the queen. The king was categorical: "Anne Boleyn is your mother. You must treat her as such." The queen was more nuanced: "I am not your mother and I never will be." This bone of contention between the king and the queen sometimes led to verbal jousts. Catherine of Aragon was declared dead or, at the very least, *persona non grata*, and the crown refused to come down on the possibility of finding a replacement for her motherly duties. The role played by Anne Boleyn in this story reminded me of Heidi's governess in Frankfurt. One day, the queen, exasperated by the discussion, settled the matter once and for all with the king: "I'll respect them, but don't ask me to love them." I was surprised to see the extent to which monarchs are prepared to do more for their people than the people are prepared to do for them. Anne Boleyn's emotions were, when you think about it, much simpler than Catherine of Aragon's. The latter could be completely irrational and unpredictable. Most of the time she was as happy as a lark, but it only took a sad song to come on the radio or a police car to drive by for her to plunge into the depths of despair. Anne Boleyn, on the other hand, responded most of the time in the same way to the same stimuli, apart from her divine rages, which she could fly into at any time for no reason at all. If slamming doors had been an Olympic discipline, the queen would have taken gold. Everything I know about the timeless art of door slamming, I learned from her.

We soon learned that she had an almost Pavlovian reflex whereby she rewarded good grades, reading progress, and signs of intelligence and general knowledge with a smile. Conversely, bad grades, misspelled words, and acts of irrational behaviour were met with disapproval and punishment. When I was seven, she explained to me that I had reached the age of reason and was now capable of thinking like an adult. In other words, I should stop whining and asking for stuff.

"Now you can understand certain things."

"Like what?"

"Things to do with people."

"People?"

"Yes. Family stuff."

From that moment on, I promised myself I would be one of those people who don't understand anything.

The unforgettable images of Nadia Comaneci's gymnastic routine the previous summer were shown again and again on TV. I thought to myself that I wanted to be free, communist, and light like her so I could fly through the air. For two years, there was no word of Catherine of Aragon. For two years, we didn't speak to her. For two years, she wasn't in the vocative case. Then one visit per year was allowed. For these eight years, we were not allowed to utter her name in the presence of the king or the queen. And the cat? I'll have to tell you about the cat soon.

Then, the same thing happened that usually happens with the twisting of memory: we took our memories underground. For the first few years of our life in Matane, the beach was somewhere to hide out and bring up her memory. The forest was too risky: you never knew who might be hiding in the bushes or who might rat on you. Very quickly, we learned never to mention in public that we were the children of this woman from Rivière-du-Loup, to never allude to her existence, to erase all memory of our love. We never even talked about it at school for fear that news of our dissent would make its way back to the queen. When a teacher, tired of teaching us spelling, suggested one May that we make a card for Mother's

Day, I said that mine was dead. In the circumstances, the idea seemed more bearable to me or at least easier than having to explain: "My mother lives in Rivière-du-Loup, I haven't seen her for two years, and I'm not allowed to talk about her. What I have just told you has put my life in danger. I'm sorry, I'm going to have to kill you." It was easier than defying Edict 101 at any rate.

So there we were on the beach. From the first lot we lived on, if you went down a big grassy hill and crossed the road you'd find us by the river. In the summer, the sand could become burning hot in the sun, despite the glacial currents that flowed down from Labrador. Reels of dried-up seaweed revealed how high the tides rose and stretched out in arcs from east to west. We found green sea urchin skeletons, blue shells, and pink tampon applicators. Sometimes we would step on a piece of glass polished by the salt. It would slide so smoothly between our fingers that we could barely imagine its sharp past. When we held it up to the sun it would look like part of a stained-glass window washed up on the beach at Matane. Coke and Pepsi bottles produced translucent shards of polished white. The green bits of glass came from 7UP bottles. Beer bottles splintered into small, dark amber pieces. On this strip of beach, the waves deposited at our feet the shattered stained-glass windows of a church sunk off the Matane coastline. My sister and I picked up the pieces without ever beginning the impossible task of putting them back together. We knew that they had once been part of a whole, but that an earthquake had probably separated them. The sea salt had made them smooth so that their edges no longer fit together. They had taken on a shape all their own. They could be traced back to a family only by their colour. A distant kinship. They had ended up where the Gulf of St. Lawrence melts into the northern blue sky, leaving ships arriving from the Atlantic in July dangling from an invisible thread. The horizon gives way to a blue void that draws the soul northward. The trip is pleasant enough. When you really let yourself go, you soar high above the gulf, the taiga, and the permafrost, until you reach the tundra, where on a sunny January day you can drift off into the light of the north.

The light from the northeast had scorched the backs of our eyes. We would never again be able to see as clearly as before. We would always have to return to the north, where the light, like an overpowering drug, dulls the senses to better assert its hold. Growing up in the dazzling light of the north condemns you to a constant search at ever-higher latitudes for this white light that cancels out the world's ugliness. Our childhood played out on an overexposed film. In blinding haziness. We would build sandcastles as tall as we were and throw the Thénardiers into their crocodile-infested moats. The poor creatures would be poisoned and float belly up on the water. It didn't take us long to work out that the sand was a giant blackboard we could write on. Unlike paper, which could at any moment be discovered at the bottom of a pocket or between two mattresses, the sand let us erase our words and pictures with a drag of the foot whenever inquisitive passersby approached. They say that during the persecutions, the first Christians would trace a fish in the sand as a sign of recognition. With the sand temple built and our limited knowledge of medieval architecture exhausted, one of the two of us would draw a sign on the beach to see what the other thought about saying a memorial mass. More often than not, we would trace an M. Other times we drew the Gaspé Peninsula, marking Matane and Rivière-du-Loup on the map. That was all we needed. We were the only two members of this outlawed sect. A creed devoted to the memory of a name. The noise of the waves covered our childish words. We sang the song of the sad dolphin, which I didn't dare sing before the king for fear he suspected it reminded me of my mother. Then, after rounding up an audience of crab carapaces, abandoned shells, and empty sea urchins, we performed our play before these dead creatures.

"Do you think she thinks about us?"

"Yes, all the time."

"Do you think she knows where we are?"

"Maybe... maybe he called her."

"Will we ever see her again?"

Hunted and distrustful. Always looking over our shoulders to make sure no one had followed us. Always making sure the wind was blowing hard enough to cover the sound of our voices. Always coming up with an alibi when asked what had kept us at the beach for so long. Sandcastles, yes, that's right, we were building sandcastles. Which wasn't entirely untrue. We built sandcastles for Micheline Raymond, professional cook, often enough. People out for a stroll who happened upon these mausoleums in our absence had no way of knowing which god they had been erected for. The high tide washed away our footsteps, castles, and memories.

We would sometimes play out scenes from our childhood in Amqui with her. My sister pretended to be her; I played myself. There were scenes from everyday life and episodes we recalled involving family members. We had to remember them all. The time when... do you remember? I remember. We could have put all these stories together to make a gospel out of them.

### She announces her return

[1]*And she said unto all of them, "I will return like a thief in the night." Much time will pass, but I will come back for you. [2]You will live apart from me for a long time, but one day, like the whale that returns to the St. Lawrence every summer, you will recognize me among them all. And one of her disciples said unto her, "Teach us to laugh like you laugh." [3]And she did say: "Laughter will come in its own time. No one will have to teach it to you. The fledgling separated from its parents grows up and learns to sing by itself. Song comes to it instinctively."*

But the gospels have their limits. Ornithologists say that birds raised in captivity without their parents only ever produce the bare bones of their song. They know the basic patterns, but can never reproduce all the subtleties. Worse still, if birds grow up with other species, they might even borrow to form their own songs. They will have a personal signature, but their song won't be exactly the same as the song of their own. That's just the way it is.

"Do you know what they told me?"

"No. What did they say this time?"

"That she wasn't clever enough to bring us up. That if she had kept us, we would have become hoodlums and idiots."

"Pfff..."

"And that our future was safe with them. That we had to look to the future. They're going to build a boat."

"A boat?"

"Yeah, a sailboat. And we're all going to sail around the world in it."

"What about school?"

"That's all they said."

"They've hidden the cat. It's ours. I don't know why they won't give it back to us."

"What cat?"

"The white cat she painted. The painting she signed. They kept it. They're hiding it."

"Where?"

"We'll find it. Don't worry."

Eventually this ritual was all we needed. It no longer had anything to do with the person to whom we were giving thanks. The funny thing about memory is that it always ends up chasing its own tail. The most important thing is to keep it moving. On this freezing, windswept beach, there was, in addition to the crab shells and sea urchins that came to our theatre, all kinds of junk. One morning we found a beached minke whale. It was still alive. We watched as it struggled to breathe beneath its own weight. We watched it die. It took hours. We were surprised to see that its mouth formed a permanent, vacuous smile, despite its suffering. Its big, black eye stared back at us, opened, closed, then closed for good. Nature did what it had to do. The whale breathed its last beneath our gaze, smiling, as though content that we had accompanied it to its death. All that was missing for the scene to go down in history was to have Maria Callas stand beside the whale on the beach at Matane and sing *La mamma morta*. The whale soon started to smell and rotted slowly on the shore. We went back every day only to discover that the birds had torn away a little more flesh from its immense, cold body. It putrefied more quickly, and its ribs appeared. Two long white ribs could be seen clearly from the road, pointing skyward. I'm sure my sister remembers the hippie who pulled up in his Volkswagen, cigarette in mouth, to tear out two of the dead whale's ribs. It took a few minutes of twisting and pulling before he could walk off with them. We later tried to tell them the story at home, but they were listening to a record and had no time for us. I think they were listening to Harmonium. You know the one... "*Où est allé tout ce monde qui avait quelque chose à raconter? On a mis quelqu'un au monde, on devrait peut-être l'écouter...*" Something about taking the time to listen to someone you brought into the world. They hummed along, looking deep into each other's eyes. Our story of the beached whale remained untold. We must have been suffering from what the English call *folie à deux*. On the beach, the hippie kept tugging away at the minke carcass. We laughed and laughed at the strange man, me with a hearty guffaw and my sister with a more muted chuckle. The laughter transformed the memory of everything into an echo.

"What are you doing?"

"I'm pulling out the whale's ribs. It doesn't need them anymore."

"What for?"

"To make sculptures."

Sculptures? I think I've seen a few of them somewhere. They're a little like elephant tusks, finely hewn and encrusted with jewels to make them more attractive. They're put on display and people think, "Wow, look at those sculpted elephant tusks. How pretty they are!" I bet that's what everyone thinks. So it must have been the same for our hippie's sculptures. He would never have been able to hide the fact that they were two whale ribs. He finally managed to rip them out to the sound of tearing flesh. My sister squeezed my hand at the horrible sound of the carnage. He left with the two bones, all smiles. Now he would be able to make his sculptures.

He would display them, and everyone would say, "How pretty they are!"

The beached whale also made me realize that I had a gift of seeing the future in animals' entrails. Since I can't get my hands on any marine mammals in the city, I sometimes read chicken and quail entrails. I can never see very clearly. Not as clearly as what the whale had to say. As it decomposed, the animal had partly revealed the future reserved for Anne Boleyn and the king. A stick was all it took to chase away the flies gathered above the carcass's guts to see the whole story. The whale shared every little detail of it with me. Curiously, there was something of a disconnect between how the king and queen imagined their future and my prophecies. Nothing they saw in the short to medium term—Quebec's separation, sailing around the world, a brighter future, the complete and utter obliteration of the memory of Micheline Raymond, professional cook—none of that appeared in the whale's entrails. I saw separation ahead, but not for Quebec. Around-the-world trips, but not on a sailboat. Forgetting, but certainly not of Micheline Raymond, professional cook. Breathless, I tried to translate into human language for Anne Boleyn the sad destiny the sea reserved for her. I found her with my father, wrapped up in the new thrill of being pregnant. Something resembling decency forced me to keep my revelations to myself. I was going to have a half-brother. "Not a half-sister?" you say. No. The child would be a boy. It was what the king and queen wanted.

An heir. It was a time for celebration, not ill omens. At any rate, Harmonium's lamentations would have stood in the way of my prophecies. *On a mis quelqu'un au monde, on devrait peut-être l'écouter... di bi di daaaaa...*

Only one thing was not washed away by the waves: the laugh she had taught us. The laugh we learned from our mother was one of our weapons of passive resistance. Our very own *Refus global*. This last sentence should be taken quite literally. My mother's laugh was a feat of nature, a work of art. It was made up of two quite complex movements. First, there was a dry and candid outburst that could knock down birds in mid-flight. Then, something approaching a contained, high-pitched cooing sound. A sonogram of her laugh would probably have been one of a kind. The laugh was too complicated for our two unpractised throats. Only Catherine of Aragon could pull it off. It was therefore tacitly agreed that I would reproduce the staccato burst and my sister would do the chuckling. And it was this laughter, our laughter, that slowly cracked the hull of the king's ship. Little by little. We couldn't talk about her, but we could laugh like her. I'm sure she had thought about it and had taught us the laugh for this very eventuality. And so we laughed, as all children laugh, and every peal of laughter, every chuckle, would draw disapproving looks. We were told not to laugh like halfwits. "Stop laughing so loudly" meant "Stop laughing like your mother." They had been caught in their own trap. It had been forbidden to utter her name in public, but not to laugh like her. Outlawing the laugh would have forced them to say her name, to mention her directly. And so my mother's laugh was our form of passive resistance. Our Bartleby. Our "I would prefer not to." With our mother's laugh, we could show the world just how happy we were, just how privileged we felt to be living in the court of King Henry VIII.

Later, years later, light was shed on the events of summer 1977. It was all very simple. Nobody had bothered to tell Catherine of Aragon that we were moving. They probably didn't want to bore her with the dull details of our mundane existence. "Family Court injunction" is also a hammer word. And it was precisely to avoid one that the king had slipped away from Rivière-du-Loup. Faced with a *fait accompli*, the rest of the world could hardly demand reparations. Which meant that the Sunday after the Great Upheaval, when she turned up in front of our house in her Renault 5, all my mother found was a huge hole crawling with worms. She told me recently that on that Sunday, she had sped her little French car along the road by the Point close to where she would bring us to eat every week. She intended to pick up enough speed to miss the turn and plunge into the sea in front of the Indian rock. But as fate would have it, the earth rumbled that day in Rivière-du-Loup, just like it does two hundred times a year. Except that day a shower of rocks broke away from the Indian's head and rolled down onto the road, causing my mother to brake suddenly. She got out of her car, looked at the Indian's head, stared it right in the eye, and marvelled, as she stood by the St. Lawrence, at how geological chaos had managed to put some order back into human chaos. She must have lit a cigarette.

Or thrown up.

One thing's for sure: at that very moment she understood exactly how much she hated the fact that everything had to fall apart. That summer, Elvis Presley died suddenly. Probably because he felt the earth shake all the way from Tennessee. It had been too much for his fragile health. Somewhere in Rivière-du-Loup, someone cried her eyes out on August 16, 1977. Like all the great queens in history, Catherine of Aragon detested unexplained disappearances.

You see, nearly two hundred times a year I feel the earth shake. Every 1.82 days. Two hundred times a year. Without fail. The little earthquakes follow me everywhere. When I'm teaching. In the shower. In the subway. On vacation. I'm only safe on a plane. So I try to travel as often as I can. Whenever my students see me clinging to the blackboard, whenever I clutch the shower head, whenever I rest my hand on the shoulder of a little old woman who looks up at me, her eyes filled with pity, it's because I'm losing my footing. I've long since stopped asking other people, "Did you feel that?" I know that my seismograph is too sensitive. For me, a four on the Richter scale is the end of the world. One day, I told a Toronto psychiatrist about it. A pharmaceutical representative had just given him some samples of small blue pills manufactured in the United States, the very thing, he said, for an affliction that's more common than the medical community would care to admit. I take one hundred milligrams of them a day. The little blue pills have made me lose a lot of weight. I prefer myself like this. They've also helped me stop shouting at strangers in the street. People prefer me like this. Even though I still feel the full force of every little earthquake, I manage to catch myself between the uneven bars. The secret is to always think one step ahead. That way, you won't fall flat on your face in a cloud of dust on the blue mat, with a disapproving Soviet judge looking on.

Boycotts and censorship force their victims to come up with alternatives. The stronger the oppression, the shrewder the ways around it have to be. This is how bonsais grow. The miniature Japanese trees are but the sum of thousands of responses to as many upsets. They are the botanical incarnation of Resistance and a miniature form of art, which also has to overcome constraints. To grow a nice bonsai, you must inflict all kinds of bearable torture on it. Never cut off too many branches. What doesn't kill it makes it more beautiful. When someone harasses or mistreats you, they are turning you into an object of beauty, a work of art. In Montreal, near the Olympic site, right beside where Nadia got her perfect score, there is a huge botanical garden. There's a small Japanese pavilion there where I like to go for walks in July. They serve green tea. There's also a beautiful bonsai exhibit. Sometimes I stop in front of the tiny trees and admire their resolve. They're sold at prices far beyond my means. The Japanese have managed to put a price on suffering and torture. You have to give them that.

The half-brother came into the world. His birth brought to light the plans that had been drawn up for us. It was quite simple: once Quebec became independent and the boat had been built, Anne Boleyn and the king would sail away with the younger brother to go live in the southern seas. Everyone was doing it back then. Anne Boleyn would educate the boy herself. My sister asked what would happen to us. Anne Boleyn replied tactfully. Bringing us along was out of the question. It was a vessel of the future, and we belonged to the past. "You? Well... It's pretty simple. You'll go off to college somewhere. And anyway, you're big enough to understand. You've reached the age of reason." It was a win-win situation for all concerned. We would study in the colleges of an independent Quebec while they zigzagged between the islands of the South Pacific. Far from incensing me, this rejection struck me as a promise of liberation. I didn't realize that my sister—may she forgive me—was saddened at being abandoned this way. I happily turned my attention to choosing my college. The very idea of being a prisoner aboard a steel ship thousands of miles away from inhabited land with only my father, Anne Boleyn, and Harmonium for company terrified me. So we would be set free at a time of their choosing. What I had taken to be a life sentence had just been commuted to barely ten years. But the whale's entrails had been categorical: separation would come much sooner. Patience was key; now wasn't the time to get ahead of ourselves. Instead, we should let things rot away and disappear by themselves. No sorrow lasts for one hundred years.

Around about the same time, the king had also begun to take an interest in local products like Atlantic cod. Fried, poached, broiled, in white sauce, and even—horror of horrors—baked whole in milk. We also ate cod liver, which we had to extract ourselves from still-wriggling fish. I remember the silver scales would stick to my forearms. Some of the smaller ones became so deeply embedded in my skin that I couldn't get rid of them. They disappeared into the depths of my epidermis only to pop up somewhere else on my body. They still reappear even today, especially during Lent, when the pale winter light brings out all of my skin's imperfections. I have to cover them up with clothes. I have lots of them behind my knees. They're smooth and shiny.

We would wash down the Matane cod with a 1977 Château Rancour. Rancour is an odourless, tasteless white wine that kills slowly. Administered early, its effects can be lifelong. We would sip a few drops every day. We had it with every meal, in the milk we dipped our cookies into after silently chewing our way through meals in the company of the king and queen. The wine made us feel better and promised happier days ahead. We realized that doubt, sadness, and melancholy could be dissolved in rancour. We quickly became addicted.

Every day we became a little more resistant. As hard as sculpted whale ribs. We still help ourselves to some on winter evenings when we have nothing better to do than remember. Whole litres that we uncork in the evening and polish off the next morning. We serve it to others, too, so they can feel its purifying effects.

Remember how we feared and hated the sordid decline of every living thing; and, while I'm on the subject, I'd also like her to know that we always showed tremendous discipline in the face of ridicule and despair.

One day, we were allowed to visit her. We had never been permitted to ask to see her. "Let her pay" was what the royal couple retorted whenever we dared ask to visit her. Pay for what? The seventeen dollars the bus ride would have cost? The king refused to pay. Later, years later, there would be attempts at rebuilding. The German language has an untranslatable adverb that perfectly describes the process: *vergeblich*. According to my Larousse bilingual dictionary, the closest French equivalent appears to be *vainement*. In vain. But this approximation, which implies vanity much too strongly, ignores the Germanic root *geben*, which means to give. *Vergeblich* means to not give oneself, to be unable to give oneself something for lack of means. I had no trouble at all learning this word years later. I had carried it within me since Matane. I had the content, all I was missing was the container. I understood it the minute I heard it. Go on, give it a try. Say *fairgabelich*. It drops with a thud, like a dead animal. I'm considering having it engraved on my headstone: "Here lies Eric Dupont, son of Micheline Raymond, professional cook. *Vergeblich.*" If someone asks me, "Sum up your life in one word," I reply, *"Vergeblich."* I can't give myself it. It's in vain. I lack the means. From my home on the Gaspé coast, unbeknownst to me I was learning German through the communicative method. All I lacked were the words. They would eventually come, like everything we promise ourselves.

We were occasionally allowed to meet her whenever we visited our grandparents, who had stayed behind in Rivière-du-Loup. With them, certain edicts fell by the wayside, to our great surprise. These visits were offered to us with breathtaking nonchalance. But we had to call her ourselves. There was no way the royal couple would enter into communications. Since my sister was petrified at the idea of speaking to our mother in front of the king and the queen, the task fell to me. She would be surprised to hear my voice. Most of the time, she hadn't even known we were in town. I oversaw the logistics of the prisoner exchange. At first once a year for a day, then more often. It went without saying that we were forbidden to talk about the visits. Especially in front of the younger brother. For years he didn't know the truth. Even the day when, one week after her second marriage—which we hadn't been invited to—our mother came to pick us up for the first time in six years at our house in Saint-Ulric, his ignorance remained intact. "Your mother will come pick you up on Saturday." Once this woman had materialized, keeping her name quiet became impossible. That which is must be named, Sister Jeannette had made that quite clear. The censors knew no bounds. We were ordered to talk about our mother like an aunt so as not to traumatize the little brother. Admirable thoughtfulness from Anne Boleyn. So she who must not be named was going to turn up in a car with her husband. In front of the little brother who might ask questions, we were to say she was an aunt. You have to admit it was an improvement on not even existing. And the cat? Oh yes, the cat!

That was in the house in Saint-Ulric, our ninth address in as many years. Just outside of Matane. Construction of the sailboat was underway. The household's entire finances were poured into it. I was as much in favour of the project as my sister was apprehensive about it. I must have been eleven, which would have made her twelve. Our faith was out of control; our laughter, sovereign. Our faith made us careless. We were daring to the point of going through their things in their bedroom, right in the heart of the court, looking for clues that would help us bring down this iron regime. The stakes were high. We couldn't allow ourselves to be caught. My sister would keep watch by the window, looking out for the square-shaped red Volvo coming in the distance, while I rifled through the wardrobe. It wasn't very well hidden. I turned the painting around and knelt before it. It was Kitty all right. She had painted it from the photograph in Amqui. A white cat in front of a white refrigerator, signed in her name. I wouldn't have swapped it for Dali's *Persistence of Memory*. I remained prostrate in silence before the cat my mother had painted for me. This scene, with my sister looking to the horizon and me kneeling before the painting, pretty much summed up our childhood. Then she would take my place in adoration before the icon. We did this a lot. One day we went up into their bedroom and discovered to our horror that the painting had disappeared. They must have thrown it out. It must have rotted in the Matane dump along with the other items that aren't deserving of a place in our homes and memories.

It was at precisely this time that I developed a fascination for the process of forgetting, like a researcher fascinated by an illness he has just discovered. Fascinated by the perfection of this thing that kills memory to allow us to live. Something inside me yelled that my memory would develop even more by learning my times tables by heart. $8 \times 7 = 56$. That I would save my mother's memory from the clutches of oblivion by learning the names of America's fifty states by heart, from west to east. *Washington, Idaho, Montana, North Dakota, Minnesota, Wisconsin, Michigan.* My encyclopedic learning rose up like a wall around this ocean of oblivion. I forced myself to remember the ten Canadian provinces (with capitals and the dates they joined Confederation), the titles of all the Tintin books, relative pronouns, subordinating conjunctions, French adjectives ending in *-ail* that become *-aux* in the plural, the Apostles' Creed, the kings of France, the names of the twelve disciples, the periodic table, all the cities that have hosted the Olympic Games since 1896, not forgetting Melbourne (1956) and Antwerp (1920), Quebec's administrative regions (my favourite to this day is *Abitibi-Témiscamingue*, you have to repeat it three times before you get it right), Canada's premiers, the names of a cow's four stomachs, Radio-Canada's broadcast schedule, and, of course, the fifteen Soviet socialist republics. No memory exercise would be complete without them. Once processed by my mind, these mountains of data translated into a simple *Micheline Raymond, professional cook* that I had to cover up with a thundering laugh. Strangely, this heap of useless information pleased the king and queen. In fact, it was the best way of attracting their attention and earning their approval.

It is reassuring to know before the age of ten that forgetting is like the universe. It expands exponentially. The speed with which it spreads increases over time. Memory, on the other hand, is limited, at least in principle. For example, whenever you gaze up at a star far, far away from Earth, it's not the star you're looking at, but an image of the star as it was billions of years ago. The further away objects are in space, the further away they are in time. Stars gradually fade and disappear. Some take longer to fade than others. In the dark skies above the Gaspé Peninsula, memory is richer than in the city. It's only when you leave the countryside that you realize with amazement that there are barely any stars left.

Hardly any memory left. The noise prevents you from seeing the memories that had seemed so clear in the country. Although seeing the Thénardier star fade away behind a cloud of smog could be the best thing that ever happened.

For a while, we kept reading and rereading Grimm, until the tales' inconsistencies moved us on to other books. In *Hansel and Gretel*, the children find their parents again after a brush with a cannibal witch's cauldron. Right up to the end, I had imagined a malevolent alliance between the witch and the children. A symbiotic union in which the witch would feed Hansel and his sister in exchange for fresh flesh they would lure back to the witch's house. This scenario in all its horror struck me as more palatable than a wholly improbable return to the parents who had left them to be eaten in the forest. To my mind, the return of Hansel and Gretel is, at once, the fairy tale's great beauty and tragic flaw.

A ghostly cat haunted the corridors of the court of King Henry VIII. The TV images of the Moscow Olympic Games showed a heftier Nadia, no longer as light as air. She had to settle for silver in the overall standings and didn't make the podium in the uneven bars. It's a demanding sport. You can't keep doing it for very long: sooner or later the body's natural development gets in the way of its movements and affects its performance.

But for a while our graceful performances on the uneven bars were of the highest calibre. I like to pretend that, just like Nadia, we got full marks for our landing on this northern beach. But marks often depend on judges who, as we all know, can sometimes be unpredictable.

I wonder if they remember the days when our laughing annoyed them so much they couldn't stand it any longer. I want my sister to laugh like that the day they bury me in the cemetery in Rivière-du-Loup. At the top of the hill overlooking the St. Lawrence. My mind is made up. Anywhere else would be unbearable. She'll lay me to rest beside my mother, with "Here lies Eric Dupont, son of Micheline Raymond, professional cook. *Vergeblich*" as an epitaph. With a little luck, she'll hear me laugh really, really loudly. Loud enough for another chunk of the Indian's head to fall onto the road and stop in its tracks a whale that has just had two ribs torn out. For the soundtrack at the funeral, I propose *La mamma morta* sung by Maria Callas, followed by *Love Me Tender* by Elvis. Anything but Félix Leclerc or Jacques Brel. If anyone dares to play *Le tour de l'île* or *Le moribond* at my funeral, I'll leap out of my coffin screaming. That would make everyone sad, and I'd rather everyone sang and was happy when they drop me in the hole. That's what the chuckle is all about, but I should really stop telling you all this. For a start, I've violated Edict 101, and there are bound to be consequences.

# CHAPTER 2

# The Brown-Headed Cowbird (1979)

SUCH WAS LIFE in the court of King Henry VIII. While the queen and king dreamed of the southern seas, I found refuge in books. Atlases were among my favourites, and to my eyes, their multicoloured maps were works of art. Then came books on popular science and animal biology. Their illustrations were a way for me to escape, if only for an instant, our depressing kingdom of the north.

Of all the animal species, those that made long annual migrations piqued my interest most. The library at the elementary school in Matane was home to quite an interesting collection on the animals of Canada. Each illustrated book focused on a particular Canadian animal, which made a change from all the books that spoke of French animals we were unlikely to ever encounter in our part of the world. What good did it do me knowing all about the reproductive habits of the hedgehog if I was condemned to live on the Gaspé Peninsula? I pounced on the "Caribou," "Moose," and "Salmon" books and devoured them with the enthusiasm others reserve for crime thrillers. Our teacher, Madame Levasseur, had noticed the quasi-religious state of ecstasy these descriptions of animal migrations plunged me into. By the spring of 1979, I had read all the books in the collection many times over. Madame Levasseur watched me comb the library shelves, desperate for anything on Canadian wildlife. Taking pity on me, she took a large book on the animals of eastern Canada out of the part of the library reserved for the older children. "You can read it over Easter break." The next day, I had already read a third of the book, which I kept beneath my pillow.

I think I secretly envied how the Canada goose and caribou could relocate twice a year with disarming ease, while I was condemned to stay behind in the court. These animal books revealed sometimes troubling behaviour from certain species of bird, including the brown-headed cowbird (*Molothrus ater*), a common enough bird in the Quebec countryside that's often mistaken for a small crow. It's not its plumage that attracts attention, but rather its reproductive behaviour. That spring, I discovered the link that bound me to this particular species. And so Madame Levasseur's book followed me everywhere I went over Easter break.

Easter will always be my favourite public holiday. I come from the north, remember. When the first Sunday following the full moon after the spring equinox rolled around, we knew the worst of winter was behind us. The ice was beginning to free the St. Lawrence—beyond which we could barely distinguish the other shore—from its annual enslavement, revealing a dazzling shade of metallic blue. And when Jesus decided to come back to life later than usual, around mid-April, the plain of frozen azure tore at the retinas of wintering residents. The deathly silence of the Gaspé countryside was shattered by the song of birds we thought we would never see again, now proclaiming their melodious return to these lands of snow. Christmas is nice: no school for two weeks. Thanksgiving isn't bad, though a little chilly. But Easter holds the promise of finding the gloves we misplaced in the January snow.

In our lost and frozen north, only the snowy owl (*Nyctea scandiaca*) interpreted the tepid western wind as a threat to its immaculate plumage and used the diversion created by the arrival of spring to take flight to the dazzling beauty of the north. This noble bird of prey, a larger cousin of the owl, captured the attention of Quebec's National Assembly in 1987 when it was made the official bird of La Belle Province. That's how things work in North America. Each tribe choses its own totems. New Jersey opted for the American goldfinch, Louisiana for the brown pelican. Recently Quebec even chose an official insect, which to everyone's surprise wasn't the mosquito. Instead, a democratic vote crowned the white admiral butterfly, which might not be very well known or particularly common, but does have pretty colours. It was a tight race against the common eastern bumblebee.

As for the snowy owl, you have to admit that the animal is a powerful symbol, a reminder not only of the splendours of winter, but also of the importance of environmental conservation. A daytime hunter, it feeds on small rodents and is particularly fond of lemmings. The snowy owl builds its nest right on the ground, an act of negligence you can't hold against it, since it reproduces at a latitude where even the hardiest spruce tree would throw in the towel. Some snowy owl couples are known to be monogamous and, year after year, they nest in the same spot and feed their young with the same affection, offering their fledglings a stable, diligent, and faithful couple for parents. You'll understand that the choice of this particular bird as the official bird of my province left me perplexed. A bird that, on clear February days, would often look down on me with a knowing air from the top of a fencepost in the fields of the Gaspé countryside, one that inspires nothing but the dignity of parental duty. What might I be implying, you ask?

It's not the first time that Quebec has been wide of the mark.

It was over Easter break that nature and propriety forced the royal court to undertake a migration of its own. Tradition had it that we would lay down our arms to speed west on the still dangerously icy roads of the Gaspé Peninsula to visit my father's parents, who lived in Saint-Antonin, a sleepy little village running along the plateau behind the town of Rivière-du-Loup. A three-hour drive along a carpet of snow. We usually set off on Good Friday morning for a three-day visit to these people of an altogether different age. Leaving Matane behind was no hardship. We were simply serving our sentence there and half my captivity was given over to planning my escape, in any case. And so I sat in the back seat of our American car, rattling off the names of the hamlets standing between us and our goal. Saint-Ulric, Baie-des-Sables, Les Boules, Grand-Métis, Sainte-Flavie, Rimouski, Trois-Pistoles, L'Isle-Verte, Cacouna, and, like one last prayer before reaching salvation, Rivière-du-Loup appeared to me like Manhattan must have appeared to the *Titanic* survivors. Some will wonder how a mere three hundred kilometres could have seemed like a return to Ithaca. Because family visits, as long as they led to Anne Boleyn's family, were so frequent they were not even announced twenty-four hours in advance. When the time came to hop aboard for these destinations, no questions were asked. My sister and I followed because that's what children do: they follow. Visits to my grandparents on our father's side, on the other hand, were limited to New Year's and Easter.

For a long time, I would sleep on car journeys. But after the Great Upheaval I tried to keep my eyes open because it turns out you can never really know where they might be taking you. Sometimes you have only to close your eyes for an hour and you can end up far from home, in distant lands not of your choosing. There was no way I was going to let that happen again. The king and queen would take me wherever they pleased, but I was at least going to know what was happening this time. It was also following the Great Upheaval that car journeys began to make me feel incredibly sick. No one has ever been able to get to the bottom of those violent, messy bouts of travel sickness. Just leaving on a trip with the king and queen was enough to turn me green. And in fact I never felt ill when I travelled with other people. The car would gather speed, the king and queen would light a cigarette at the same time, and less than ten minutes later I would already be green in the back seat, much to the displeasure of the queen, whose tone would become reproachful. Sometimes they would have to stop the car and let me vomit at the side of the road while the queen cursed, "Are you done? What's taking you so long?" My sister was less given to these moments of weakness than I. Burying my nose in a book would help me delay the inevitable by a minute or two, which meant that I would be sick after Rimouski and not before. I would bury my nose in my book again to forget my vomiting spell.

According to that same book, the brown-headed cowbird owes its name to its habit of following herds of cows across the farms of North America. Before it followed cows, the cowbird would follow buffalo across the plains, back when it was still called a buffalo bird. Which means that it has never had a name of its own; it's always been named after the animal it follows. The book also explained that the bird doesn't build a nest. Just like the cuckoo, it squats in the nests of other birds to lay its eggs.

My reading was often interrupted by the king pointing out something by the side of the road. Near Rimouski there was, for instance, a big sign for "Monkey Heaven" a few kilometres to the south. The image of monkeys fresh out of the equatorial forest had the power to surprise on these boundless snow-covered stretches of highway. The place was a little like a zoo, but with only monkeys. They lived behind big windows, locked up year round in narrow wooden cages. Visitors would file past the filthy vivariums, home to a handful of sad and panic-stricken baboons looking around for their native Africa. The king explained that the place had been shut down after the authorities received a number of complaints about mistreated monkeys. They were underfed, they got sick, and they were left to die in their grimy cages. The crime appalled me. But I went on with my reading to keep my travel sickness at bay. The book went into great detail on the bird's parasitic reproductive behaviour. In the spring, the female cowbird lays an egg in another species' nest. The other mother often doesn't suspect a thing and sits on the intruder's egg along with her own. I was beginning to nod off in the back seat. Sleep slowly got the better of me, triggering terrible nightmares populated by starving monkeys and parasitic cowbirds. Books and reality intertwined, and I dreamed I was flying, beating my wings high above Virginia and Massachusetts, heading for Canada. The king woke me up when we arrived at my grandparents' village.

Saint-Antonin looks like any one of the hundreds of church-spired villages scattered across Quebec. The difference being that the municipality of Saint-Antonin (the village *and* parish) had a strange bylaw: bores were not tolerated. At the entrance to the village, a kindly guard leaned his head into each car to be sure it didn't contain anyone on his list. It was like a scene out of the Soviet Union. The guards had an almost infallible technique for sniffing out stuffed shirts. As the car slowly pulled up to the sentry box, one of the guards would follow the other's every movement, like the mime artists who practice their art in shopping malls. When the first guard realized what he was up to, he would turn and slap him hard across the face. A ferocious battle royal ensued.

If the people inside the car began to laugh, the barrier was raised immediately to let them through. If they remained impassive in the face of such antics, their identity was checked. Such searches had been known to take hours. If, by some misfortune, they took it into their heads to step out of the car to explain to the second guard that it wasn't right to make fun of others, and to the first that it was bad manners to slap his colleagues, their vehicle was refused passage on the spot. The license plate number was recorded in a surprisingly thick register and the information sent to the other villages around the world with similar legislation. An updated list of bores went out each year. Individuals named on it either had to refrain from visiting Saint-Antonin or do so incognito, keeping a low profile all the while. Whenever the border guards caught an intruder in the hamlet, they marched him or her to the village limits, explaining politely but firmly the reason for their expulsion. In Saint-Antonin's defence, the whole atmosphere in the village was at stake. We had uncles and aunts who had to be protected from pain-in-the-neck visitors. Not that they weren't able to protect themselves, but keeping outsiders at bay is tiresome and there is an infinite number of them. Some might cry xenophobia or intolerance. But to me it's just basic common sense. If you're a bore, you have a choice: shut up or stay home.

Entering my grandparents' house was like an Acadian homecoming, with shouts of joy, tearful hugging and kissing, and sparkling eyes. My grandmother, a woman who could make up for all of human iniquity with a single smile, the woman I would point to without the slightest hesitation if ever aliens kidnapped me and asked which human being should come with me to the planet Serenity, the woman who for years covered my fingers with wool during our harsh winters, would be waiting for us in a home so tidy it was the envy of Anne Boleyn. If it's true that cleanliness is next to godliness, my grandmother's house must have been the Vatican's anteroom. Once she stopped bustling about long enough to finally sit down in her rocking chair, we could see, if we squinted hard, particles of kindness dancing around her head. One day, the spiral of existence will cause these elementary particles of kindness to leave their orbit for a headlong dash into the void. That day, with a little luck, one of them will hit me square in the chest and transform me into an acceptable human being.

Before getting out of the car, the king and queen quickly took off their crowns and hid them in the trunk. All royal privileges were lost at my grandparents' house. Another reason to enjoy these visits to Saint-Antonin was that I no longer felt the little earthquakes there. It was quite amusing really. Henry VIII spoke to his father and mother as though they were gods. We found it hilarious. My grandmother, the happy woman that she was, was in raptures from the moment we arrived. She welcomed with open arms her two little soldiers on leave, her grown-up Henry VIII and his companion (whom she defused with a single glance), and my half-brother, still too much of a half to gauge the depths of the well of happiness we had just fallen into. We had been reduced to refugees, fleeing some country or other of misfortune and raised voices. The transformation was complete. We became planets orbiting around my grandmother. No Château Rancour flowed in her home. "How are the roads? Do you have much snow over your way? How big you all are! How good-looking, too! I'm so happy to see you!" She spoke an Esperanto understood by all, a language that used prosaic questions to give each of us back our value as human beings. There were no edicts in this house. The sabres returned to their sheaths, the cannons fell silent, the mines were deactivated. The series of offerings could begin.

Back then my grandmother used to sing along to a Gilles Vigneault album she was especially fond of. In all objectivity, her rendering of *Les gens de mon pays* was much more convincing than the original. A beer would suddenly appear, never turned down by my father, and soft drinks flowed freely, setting off a much more serious discussion of the burning issues of the day. A heartless neighbour had put up a damned shortwave antenna, scrambling the radio reception, much to the chagrin of my grandmother, who liked to fill her home with music. A lamb my grandfather was raising in the shed behind the house now weighed over forty pounds. My great-aunt Jeannette from Manitoba had written a letter warning us not to seed too early, a warning that had to be taken quite literally since everyone knows that Canada's west is the testing ground for the seasons in the east. And so we learned, without having to say a word, the teachings required to survive this land: beware your neighbours, the ideal weight of a sacrificial lamb is close to forty pounds, and summer comes from Manitoba. After these initial lessons, it was time to sit down at the table, on grandfather's orders, before we collapsed with hunger. The table was besieged, and the barley soup just waiting to be served and gobbled up.

Since we're already up to our haunches in folklore, allow me to let you in on a little secret: before turning to farming, my grandfather was a lumberjack. One day in Germany, I said that to a table of very well-dressed people eating fries. *Mein Großvater war Holzfeller.* They laughed. I don't think they believed me. It was too much. And yet the photographic proof exists. There is a photo of him somewhere in the snow, on a horse the foremen gave him for chopping down a record number of trees.

Apart from on New Year's Day, when we asked my grandfather to bless us, he never felt compelled to stoop so low as to speak. We knew him as a big softie who bawled with emotion on New Year's at the sight of us all together or who cried his heart out because one of his sons had missed the occasion. His big failing was a love for the god of plenty. Visits to him had to be made on an empty stomach. "EAT!" was an order to be obeyed, even on your deathbed. My grandfather was an eater. Calories were his ultimate goal. Hunger was a priority, and his every action was dictated by the next meal. People said he got that way after growing up hungry in a very poor family, where supper often consisted of a boiled turnip shared between seven. The turnip had usually been stolen from a neighbour's field and was chewed in frustrated silence. My great-grandfather eventually wound up buying a plot of land and some animals, bringing the food shortage to an end. Since I first heard the story, eating turnip has become akin to partaking in the Eucharist for me. I eat turnip like Jews eat matza, the unleavened bread that Moses ordered them to prepare before leaving Egypt, to remember harder times. I eat turnip in solitude and in darkness. Its bitter taste and slightly stringy consistency are nothing but a polite reminder that I am only one generation removed from hunger. I usually eat it during Holy Week. Every bite turns my stomach, but I finish my plate in silence. Sometimes I even go back for seconds, which I eat pinching my nose and with tears in my eyes, in memory of the bleak land that is eastern Quebec. One day, some folks from Montreal, very educated, very kind anglophones, invited me round to eat. It was a fancy lunch in the rich part of town. Four courses. It was, if I'm not mistaken, also Good Friday. A few repugnant chunks of turnip floated in the soup. Extreme poverty had managed to sneak its way into the homes of Westmount to remind me of something or other. To work, to never give up, certainly, but more importantly that life would never let me forget that my grandfather went hungry. That I would carry this hunger within me for all eternity. That it would never be sated. That every meal offered only brief respite from the burning pain of the starving man. Each little piece tasted of destitution. The turnip is particular in that it whets the appetite of those who eat it. To eat turnip is to eat humanity and all its suffering.

My grandfather, a carpenter by trade, had learned that it was best to keep farm animals on this barren land. First he raised cattle like everyone else, then when his children started to leave the family home, he got rid of the farm. Although he did keep a shed for the chickens, rabbits, and occasional lamb until he could no longer move around easily. He showed off his animals with pride and clung to them desperately. They no doubt reassured him when he saw prices go up at the supermarket. He was aware of his dependence on them. The rest of the family explained to us that he kept this harmless little farm for want of anything better to do, to find work for idle hands. That seemed unlikely to me. He could just as easily have carved dining-room furniture out of wood, grown vegetables, or gone off on his moped to pick berries along the country roads, all favourite pursuits of his. Instead, my grandfather looked after his farm animals and tended a vast garden after the trauma of famine. A man who was once hungry for days hankers for the company of chickens and rabbits. Where others saw feathers and fur, he saw a meal. For him, there was no such thing as leisure time. It was all about calories. For him, the Saint-Jean-Baptiste Day parade signalled the start of berry-picking season. He picked strawberries in June, raspberries in July, and blueberries in August. Bucketfuls that my grandmother made into pies and jams. He had no time for tourism, sport, music, or any of the other things that put nothing on his plate or were simply a distraction from calorie production. Every spring, my grandmother would have to beg and cajole him to let her take over two small rows in the garden where she could grow her gladioli. "If not for him, I'd plant flowers everywhere and get rid of the vegetables altogether," she confided in me. He looked down on her gladioli and would go on and on about how you can't eat flowers, as he angrily hoed between his yellow beans.

It was nice to see him work. We admired him, not only for his enthusiasm and steadfast determination to be at one with nature, but because he didn't even have all his fingers. He had lost four or five of them, playing with dynamite by all accounts. It came as a surprise the first time you saw his maimed hands. Then, as we got to know him, my sister and I came up with all kinds of cockamamie reasons why he might have lost his fingers. He had lost them in a war. A rival had cut them off in a battle. A wolf had torn them off in a fight to the death. He had fallen asleep on a railway track. The idea of my grandfather "playing" with dynamite as a child surprised me. I had never thought of dynamite as a toy before. I secretly envied my grandfather for having lived through wild times, back when you were allowed to have fun with explosives.

Sometimes, some unfortunate soul would visit my grandfather for a very special form of treatment. He knew how to rid the body of warts, you see. I never saw him in action, but it seems that he spoke to them quietly to persuade them to leave. I have no data on the effectiveness of his approach. Patients nevertheless continued to show up at his door. I often amuse myself imagining what he might have been saying to the warts. I came up with all kinds of lines, from the vulgar to the poetic. A healer, a carpenter, a farmer, and a prankster, my grandfather made up for his lack of education by never boring a soul.

It was a happy coincidence that our Easter visits always coincided with the sugaring-off season. While we were there, young countryfolk would often ring the doorbell to offer us maple products at rock-bottom prices. My grandfather would then set down his pipe on his ashtray mounted on a moose leg (I think Henry VIII might have killed the animal out hunting one day), stand up, and break his silence. The little salesgirl, inevitably a very distant relation of ours, would leave the house twenty dollars richer. He would buy maple syrup, taffy, and butter indiscriminately. Then he would sit me down with my sister on a bench, put the small end of a huge funnel in our mouths, and empty into them the entire contents of his purchase. "Eat!" He didn't care if it was eleven in the morning or two in the afternoon. I suspect he lost sleep worrying that my sister and I might be going hungry. He took "I'm full, thanks" to mean "I'd love another four slices, with potatoes if there are any left."

Sitting with my book in my grandparents' living room, I learned that the cowbird's eggs are sometimes chucked out of the nest. The opposite is also possible. Sometimes the squatter, once hatched, gets rid of the other eggs by puncturing them. The little parasite nestling, often bigger than the others, eats the food destined for its adoptive brothers and sisters, effectively starving them to death. I looked at the king and queen in my grandfather's company. I wondered if there were any cowbirds in Saint-Antonin. There had to be, according to the map in my book. They must arrive by the dozen every spring. In the Saint-Antonin forest, there must have been many nests with squatters in them. Soon, pairs of warblers, jays, and buntings would be discovering unknown eggs in their nests, eggs that they would decide to either keep or get rid of. The travel sickness was gone now. The sound of washing-up in the kitchen brought me back to reality, far from birds that relied on others to raise their young.

The table was set, and no one was going to turn down Grandma's humble invitation to sit down for "nothing special." Back then, she still cleaned the local branch of the credit union every morning, while my grandfather's broad farmer's body occupied the rocking chair that looked out over the St. Lawrence Plain. We imagined that during the two hours it took Grandma to dust the credit union (*Le souci de l'épargne épargne les soucis*, it said, on the tiny pencils she gave us), nothing worth writing home about ever happened in the house. But that particular Good Friday made us realize we should treat calm and silence with the wariness normally reserved for tax returns.

That Good Friday, we found my grandfather home alone. Before inquiring about our health, the state of the roads, or the weather over in Trois-Pistoles, he of course wanted to know if we were hungry. Grandma still wasn't back from the credit union and had asked him to stir the soup and wait for us. Simple enough instructions, but not the type you give to a prankster like him.

The soup was ready by the time my grandmother got back. We were waiting for her to come home before we sat down to eat. I have no recollection of my grandfather handling kitchen utensils, nor of the important place that Catherine of Aragon had occupied in his heart, a place that none of the string of women my father had paraded in front of him over the years had ever managed to win over. Perhaps that affection had stemmed from the fact that my grandfather and my mother worked together at different ends of the calorie supply chain? He in production and she in processing. Was he, too, aware of the risks associated with uttering her name? What I was told years later was that he was very fond of Micheline Raymond, professional cook. She had lived with them back when she was very young, and pregnant with my sister. After the birth of this first child, my mother had stayed in Saint-Antonin with Henry VIII for a while. An acrylic painting of a spray of flowers hung on the living-room wall, a sign of the time my mother spent in my grandparents' life. It was there. It would have been burned in Matane. It was signed "Micheline" in black. Censored art in my grandma's living room.

The soup went down slowly and noisily. Barley soup, it was. The dish that transcends all social classes. The soup that's served on Tuesday afternoons and on

Christmas Day alike. The soup that soothes an entire country. And the preparation that went into barley soup, that, too, bordered on the sacred in our house.

Steam rose from the soup pot. My grandmother's clock struck twelve. She arrived just in time for the meal, delighted to be served for once by her husband. We reached the bottom of the first bowl. Everyone complimented my grandmother's soup. Even though we ate the same soup all the time in Matane. Henry VIII was respectfully submissive in front of his parents, which was touching to see. Anne Boleyn, for her part, was all "Madame" this and "Monsieur" that, language usually reserved for official protocol. When she finished her bowl, she nibbled on a meat-covered bone. "The chicken is delicious." Grandma bristled. "Chicken in my soup?" Anne Boleyn wondered if she had mistaken the animal. "What do you mean, chicken in my soup? On Good Friday?" Back in 1979, serving chicken on Good Friday in a respectable household in Saint-Antonin was akin to serving ham sandwiches with mustard (non-kosher mustard) at a Jewish funeral reception. Anne Boleyn was left with the unpleasant impression she had said something foolish. Grandma flew into a panic. She jumped up, dashed into the kitchen, grabbed the saucepan, poked around with a ladle, and, to her horror, discovered a piece of meat. The ladle fell from her hand. Grandad, meanwhile, winked broadly at my sister and me and gave us a sly smile. The cheek of it! In the argot of pranksters, a wink meant that an atomic bomb was about to be dropped. Grandma wanted to know *right this minute* what a piece of meat was doing in the soup. This was no laughing matter. There had better be a good explanation. Henry VIII and Anne Boleyn set down their spoons. I went on eating. The king smiled awkwardly. He knew his father, and what was coming wouldn't be pleasant. For some, at any rate.

The presence of poultry in the barley soup that Good Friday, 1979, was explained to us in an old patois that is no longer spoken. Grandad laughed as he spoke. He was relying on two thousand years of patriarchy, which forbade any questioning of a father's decision. It was quite simple. He had been rocking himself as he waited for us, looking out over the plain, slightly bored. But, as you know, boredom is not permitted in Saint-Antonin. A bird with iridescent feathers was perched on the washing line. Grandad decided to take out his shotgun. He took down the bird in the middle of its Good Friday chirruping. The bird was plucked and cleaned. Then popped into the barley soup to cook, flying in the face of every precept of the Holy Catholic Church. So there you had it, that was the Quiet Revolution. It was my grandfather who insisted on serving Anne Boleyn a wing from the brown-headed cowbird. This was a man who, for his whole life, rejected the metric system and degrees centigrade, to remind us all where we came from. He was Charles Baudelaire's owl who refused to move.

Now, I can hear you asking all the usual questions. "Given that it was raised by parents of a different species, doesn't the brown-headed cowbird suffer from an identity problem?" Not in the slightest. Raised in the nest of an American yellow warbler, it grows up with parents who don't look the least bit like it. While its feathers aren't suddenly going to turn yellow, you could be forgiven for expecting it to at least try to sing like its adoptive parents in a kind of tribute to them. You might think it would learn from the American yellow warbler and build a nest for its own young. But no. The brown-headed cowbird does none of those things. It leaves the nest one day and never comes back. On its travels, it meets other young cowbirds who have also abandoned their adoptive families. They strike up an instant rapport. They form groups. All summer long, they terrorize the fields of Saint-Antonin. And at the first hint of a nip in the air, they head south, flying over Maine, New Hampshire, Massachusetts, Connecticut, New York, New Jersey, Pennsylvania, and Maryland to spend their winters with like-minded brown-headed cowbirds on the lawns of Baptist churches. If, quite by chance, they were to happen upon the warblers that raised them, they wouldn't so much as bat an eye. The brown-headed cowbird isn't a creature of sentiment. That's all Madame Levasseur's book had to say about the brown-headed cowbird. I admired and respected that bird.

Some American researchers recently managed to explain how the brown-headed cowbird continues to ruin the lives of its victims. Because sometimes the host birds do, in fact, spot the intruder and fling the egg down onto the ground. But what the researchers discovered is that, after laying their eggs, the cowbirds keep a close eye on the warblers' movements. If they dare destroy the cowbirds' eggs, their nests are ransacked. And so to avoid this happening, the host birds have no choice but to sit on the cowbirds' eggs, feed their young, and raise them as their own.

*Jesus of Nazareth* always played on television on Good Friday afternoons. My grandmother would let us watch it in peace until three o'clock. Then we had to observe a minute's silence for Christ who died on the cross. "He died on the cross at three o'clock on the dot," she would tell us, turning off the television set just as Jesus was healing a blind man. I still wonder where she got that from and if that would be three o'clock in Greenwich, Jerusalem, or Saint-Antonin. I imagine faith transcends time zones. We kept quiet. Then, for a minute, we heard nothing but the reassuring tick-tock of the cuckoo clock. It reminded me of a Jacques Brel song: a clock that says yes, that says no, that's waiting for us. I stared at the painting by Micheline Raymond, professional cook, thinking of Anne Boleyn being sick in the toilet, of the Virgin Mary in tears on Calvary, of the brown-headed cowbird on the washing line, and of the birds that were forced to raise the offspring of others on pain of having their nests ransacked. Looking at the spray of flowers my mother had painted, I kept saying to myself that all reigns come to an end one day, that cooks and simple countryfolk make natural allies, and that I really must learn to make barley soup. Cod scales continued to appear behind my knees, but I wasn't so worried about it now. I was beginning to reconcile myself to chaos. And coming up with prayers of my own... Lord, forgive mischievous grandfathers for they know not what they do.

One day, my grandfather died. He silently withdrew from the world. It was snowing when we laid him to rest. The snow suited him perfectly. He had come into the world in February, and winter had taken him from us. It was just before Christmas. I swore that day to become just as mischievous and just as fat as he had been. I work on it every day. It's an exhausting regimen. I should manage it by the age of fifty, if I'm spared. I also want it to be snowing when I'm buried. I know you can't just order such things on demand, but you can always hope. Hope. That's what we learned on that particular Good Friday. Isn't that right, sis?

# CHAPTER 3

# The Winkle (1981)

ON OCCASION, a mollusc will roll along a beach on the Gaspé Peninsula and shine its light on the shadows of humankind. That is how the winkle, a little edible marine gastropod, came into my life just as I was preparing for the Holy Sacrament of Confirmation. If, on a winter's night, a traveller should stop in one of the frozen villages along the Gaspé coastline—one of the villages with a silver church spire that pierces the northern sky, where, come evening, the waves can be heard lapping at the huge blocks of ice washed up on the shore—he would experience a moment of polar silence that would remind him of the troubling existence of God. Were he to knock on any given door, any one at all, he might be invited inside to warm up. With a little luck, he'd be offered a bite to eat. The lady of the house, sometimes known as the queen of the household, would take a huge jar of molluscs in brine out of the fridge. But behind this innocent offering was a vocabulary test designed to judge the visitor. We should all know how to behave in such a situation, because a single word will tell you more about yourself than any autobiographical novel filled with truths and half-truths.

The savvy traveller will exclaim, "Oh! *Bigorneaux*!" which will earn him a smile of approval and perhaps a friendly correction: "We call them *borlicoccos* around here." You might also say, without fear of reprisal, "*Bourgots*!" which, while not zoologically correct, at least has the merit of being understood by the locals. But someone who fails to do their homework before setting out may think they're "*escargots de mer*": sea snails. And in this case, it is possible that the local woman, a smile playing at the corners of her mouth, will correct the stranger. Because the sea snail simply does not exist in the French language. It's a name that was invented for educational purposes to refer to a marine mollusc as opposed to its land-based counterpart. A sea snail no more exists in French than does a *cheval de mer*: a sea horse. It's perfectly comprehensible, but you should say *hippocampe* instead. And a visitor who takes his research a shade too seriously could announce, with some pride, that he loves eating *Littorina littorea*, the winkle's awkward scientific name. In this particular case, the woman of the house will reply "Eating *what*?!"

looking the stranger right in the eye. You see, no one, except perhaps for a handful of socially challenged classicists, would ever order *Gadus morhua*; everyone eats cod. Your Latin prowess will impress no one here. Also, be sure to avoid *"vignot,"* unless you want to pass for a Norman washed up on the Gaspé shoreline. The terms *"bigorneau commun," "bigorneau gris,"* and *"bigorneau anglais"* may be perfectly accurate and accepted by the Canadian Wildlife Service, but such a degree of precision is unnecessary for the conversation at hand. *"Buccin"* is also best avoided. *Buccins* are much smaller than *bigorneaux*. They're used in *buccin*-spitting contests, which involve sucking the *buccin* into your mouth right out of the shell and spitting it as far as possible. The sport is practiced largely in the French departments of Brittany and Charente-Maritime. A tourist over from Belgium might say *"caricoles,"* while an Englishman would be delighted to see some "whelks." A Laotian immigrant, fresh off the boat, probably wouldn't say anything at all. Laotians who turn up on the Gaspé Peninsula are rarely talkative, as this story will show.

Even though there was a winkle-processing plant in Matane, the king and queen never brought any home. Apparently, there was a limit to their love of fresh local products. We know very little of the winkle's behaviour. And, truth be told, it is of interest to virtually no one. The animal stirs no romantic feelings, no curiosity, unless it finds itself on a plate. In this respect, the winkle confirms Aristotle's classification of the animal kingdom, in that it is only of interest because it can be eaten. And yet I suspect it might harbour unusual intentions, as this story may yet reveal.

We were living, back then, at our ninth address, in the countryside close to Matane, on Saint-Ulric's rural route number four. We were on our fourth elementary school and living in the second house that Henry VIII had built with his own hands, in the style of a typical Quebec home. A case of looking to the future while acknowledging the past? The king was going through a period of reconciliation with his architectural and culinary heritage. Needless to say, cod was part of this trend and we ate it in copious amounts. The year 1981 had a distinctly maritime flavour.

When I was eleven years old, the entire court moved into this home in Saint-Ulric. As per the province's education act, my sister and I were sent to the village school, as though to signal that we weren't quite at the end of the world. I ended up in the class of Madame Nordet, a long-time teacher and devout Catholic.

In my class there was a strapping tomboyish girl by the name of Nathalie, whose parents bred horses. She spoke very loudly and was given to bouts of explosive laughter. I was in grade four. That spring day when I walked into my new class in Saint-Ulric, the teacher asked me to read a passage from a book to see what level I was at. I made every effort, as Sister Jeannette had taught me, to articulate each syllable and give every sentence a sense of rhythm. The good nun would have been so proud to see that her lessons had borne fruit. My reading was flawless. Nathalie, however, found my lisp ridiculous and said as much. "He talks with the tip of his tongue!" she shouted, when my performance was over, giving an especially ugly laugh. A chain reaction ensued. She had wanted to put me in my place for daring to show my culture. That day, from an ill-lit corner of the classroom, there came for the first time the terse and destructive condemnation I was to hear several times a week for years on end, right up until I left the Gaspé Peninsula for good. *Faggot*. A cutting, scathing put-down, delivered in a tone that contained all the contempt in the world. There seemed to be no way to shake this label. I didn't know what a faggot was, but I knew I didn't want to be one. I was serving the sentence before having committed the crime.

Before I came to Saint-Ulric, I had a soft spot for mature ladies who wore a cross around their necks. Madame Nordet helped develop my understanding of the world. She told us in September that we were to immediately begin preparing for confirmation, which would be held in the springtime, a little after Easter, to coincide more or less with Pentecost. The ceremony was to confirm—as the name suggests—the promises I had made at my baptism, three weeks after being born, in the church in Amqui. I tried in vain to recall the ceremony on July 11, 1970. What had I pledged to do? A certificate of baptism, which the king took great care of and which I had to produce on many an occasion, proved that the baptism had indeed taken place. The document provided my mother's name, a quirk of history in the court of Henry VIII. And now I was to go through the whole rigmarole all over again. This time we would have to learn songs, read countless stories, and practice a meticulously planned ritual for months on end, with the Holy Spirit playing the leading role. Throughout the ceremony, tongues of fire would descend from heaven to bring us knowledge and wisdom. In short, we were going to recreate the miracle of Pentecost on a smaller scale on the Gaspé coast. It was against this liturgical backdrop that a crack began to form in the concrete faith in the Church that Sister Jeannette had instilled in me. It all began with an attempt to illustrate the gospels. One day, Madame Nordet asked us to use our pencil crayons to draw the following scene:

**19** *And Jesus entered and passed through Jericho.*
² *And, behold, there was a man named Zacchaeus, which was the chief among the publicans, and he was rich.*
³ *And he sought to see Jesus who he was; and could not for the press, because he was little of stature.*
⁴ *And he ran before, and climbed up into a sycamore tree to see him: for he was to pass that way.*
⁵ *And when Jesus came to the place, he looked up, and saw him, and said unto him, 'Zacchaeus, make haste, and come down; for today I must abide at thy house.'*
⁶ *And he made haste, and came down, and received him joyfully.*

*[7] And when they saw it, they all murmured, saying that he was gone to be guest with a man that is a sinner.* (Luke 19, 1-7)

Yes, Jesus stayed with Zacchaeus. At Zacchaeus's stayed Jesus. Readers at this point may wish to repeat the last two sentences three times and have a good laugh. The story aimed to show us that Jesus was accessible to even the littlest amongst us. I liked the idea. Although I didn't consider myself "little," I often wondered if having reached the age of reason and being old enough to understand certain things meant that I was worthy of attention in the eyes of Jesus. I poured every talent I had into the Jericho scene. The houses didn't pose much of a problem since I had seen them in other depictions of the gospels. White squares with flat roofs and wooden beams. Nothing too hard about that. Zacchaeus and Jesus weren't too difficult either. Two white, rectangular tunics with a thick beard on top and a haircut like the singers from Harmonium in the 1970s. Child's play. The sycamore gave me trouble, though. "Madame Nordet, what's a sycamore?" Madame Nordet was sometimes irritated by my questions. Once I had asked her if Jesus might simply have walked across a frozen stretch of lake to confound his apostles. "Impossible!" she replied. "Lakes do not freeze in the Holy Land!" She may well have been right. As for my sycamore, she told me it was a very large, multicoloured tree, which didn't help me very much. Multicoloured? Did she mean blue, red, and violet or orange, yellow, and red? For fear of creating a monstrous hybrid species, I decided instead to draw a tall maple for Zacchaeus. I had only to look out into the schoolyard to see my model. I gave the holy drawing my all. I had to resharpen the same wooden pencils several times and concentrate fully, forgetting everything around me. The maple would be so beautiful that people would come from Rome to see it. The bishops of Canada would be so amazed they'd ask the pope to have the gospels amended to refer to a maple, not a sycamore, from then on. New believers would imagine Zacchaeus perched on the branch of a huge maple tree, not in a tree that had such a strange name we had trouble drawing it. Lost in these spirals of artistic creation, possessed by the spirit of Zacchaeus—a man I would identify with for years to come—it was a near-mystic experience for me. My drawing surpassed my every expectation. I showed it proudly to Madame Nordet. She gave it a distracted glance and said, sounding clearly disappointed, that my sycamore looked more like a maple. I reminded her that I had asked her what a sycamore looked like and all she had said was that it was a large, multicoloured tree.

"I didn't say it was a maple."

"Have you ever seen a sycamore?"

"Um, no!"

"Well, how can you say my tree's not a sycamore then?"

Madame Nordet was offended and unamused at my line of questioning. She knocked off a few points for

108

failing to follow instructions and ordered me to go sit back down with my maple tree. I was so insulted that she had rejected what I considered to be the world's finest depiction of a maple that I decided that, from that moment on, I would have the apostles wear scarves and wristwatches and fly jet planes in the skies over Palestine as a backdrop to the feeding of the multitudes.

Something told me that Madame Nordet was mistaken. When I got home, I headed straight for my dictionary to be clear in my own mind. The definition for sycamore read: "A type of European maple tree with five-pointed leaves." It was a bitter victory. Zacchaeus had, in fact, been perched on the branch of a Palestinian maple. Sometimes the scriptures can miss the point altogether.

The affair hadn't diminished in the least my resolve to prepare for my confirmation with all the ardour required by the Holy Sacrament. My first communion had left me a little revolted because it felt so close to cannibalism. My first confession, which had also taken months to prepare for, I had also found trifling. Was I really going to own up to thoughts of regicide to a stranger in the half-light? Confirmation, on the other hand, with all its pomp and circumstance, filled me with inspiration. And the songs they were teaching us were much better than any we had known before. Apart from Extreme Unction, now all that remained on the Church's program of sacraments were marriage or holy orders. I wasn't planning on either. Somehow I managed to confuse the arrival of the archbishop, who was to preside over the ceremony, with the arrival of the Holy Spirit. The old gentleman was coming up from Rimouski, and this was not the time for a single false note. I don't think we could have done more had we been welcoming the pope himself. In 1981, the Holy Spirit was an old man, up from Rimouski.

There is a photograph of me and my sister with the archbishop of Rimouski. I think my sister has it. The holy man, once every two years, embarked on a spring-time tour that took him hundreds of kilometres from the seminary in Rimouski to honour all the children along the Gaspé coastline with a little slap on the face on the occasion of their holy confirmation. Route 132 became one long rosary for him, every bead a village along the way. While this travelling dove experienced the mystery of the Pentecost four times a week every spring, for us the ceremony was well and truly unique. A simple priest had sufficed for baptism, communion, and confession. But for something as serious as the bestowal of the Holy Spirit, a higher rank was required. Given the uniqueness and singular nature of this event, the communion preparations seemed like insignificant babbling in comparison to the preparation that went into the ceremony. Even today, when things are quiet, I sometimes find myself humming the theme music in the most surprising circumstances. When I'm doing the dishes. Scouring the bath. *Come Holy Spirit, come. Come Holy Spirit, come and live in us today.* As soon as we went back to school in September, the grade five and six teachers, eager to show the archbishop what they were made of when it came to matters pastoral, launched into a program to prepare us for confirmation that taxed our young minds as much as preparing for the bar would have done. Eager to please, I yielded to the degrading exercise, learning hymns and prayers by heart, if only to irritate the king and queen.

All the fuss and bother began with the launch of a little wooden boat on the St. Lawrence River and ended with an evening bordering on the satanic, in the candle-lit interior of the Saint-Ulric parish church. We had ordered the half-metre-long boat from a village artisan, who fashioned it in the image of the cargo ships we saw pass by from east to west every day, and then from west to east. Our little boat was a carbon copy of the *Hudson Transport*, a cargo ship that caught fire on the Christmas Day before I started fifth grade. Panicked by the flames, the frightened sailors decided to try their luck in a lifeboat, but unfortunately it flipped over on its way down into the water. The sailors tumbled head-first into the icy water of the Gulf of St. Lawrence, succumbing to hypothermia in less than ten minutes. The news left the king pensive. The queen was far from reassured by the whole affair. You see, they had begun work on the steel sailboat that was to whisk them off to their tropical dream, and the incident left them feeling jittery. The men who decided to stay aboard the *Hudson Transport* and fight the flames were all rescued by a Coast Guard helicopter. The incident, which I didn't see for myself since it took place several kilometres offshore, marked me for life. It was especially upsetting that the drowned sailors disappeared beneath the ice. The Coast Guard never managed to recover the bodies. I was an eyewitness to this part of the story, though. The police were called every time a body appeared, in all kinds of circumstances. Suicides, accidents, murders, lightning strikes, drownings... it was often Henry VIII who had to deal with them. Sometimes he would describe to us over supper just how putrid the bodies smelled.

The sinking of the *Hudson Transport* and preparations for my confirmation coincided with a family of Asian refugees coming to Saint-Ulric. One day, Madame Nordet announced that we would soon have in our midst a student who didn't speak French. Saint-Ulric would be welcoming a large family from Laos. Laos, she explained, was a country beside Vietnam, bordered by the Mekong. Bloodthirsty communists (another hammer word) had seized power and were persecuting all those who remained faithful to the king, as well as anyone they didn't like the look of. The suffering endured by these poor folk was recounted to us in great detail. Laos, a former French colony, had fallen under the heel of the USSR and had become no place to live. The Canadian government had agreed to take in a number of Laotian refugees and, killing two birds with one stone, made some of them take up residence in the outermost reaches of Quebec, like the Gaspé Peninsula, for at least four years. That way, integration would be easier, and regions that were becoming dangerously depopulated would be given a demographic shot in the arm from the immigration ministry. The logic behind the operation was far from subtle: "No one seems to want to have anything to do with the Gaspé Peninsula anymore. But you don't have much choice, so you'll have to make do. Welcome to Canada."

I found the whole undertaking extraordinarily romantic. The villagers of Saint-Ulric spent weeks tracking down everything required for a happy household. The people who would soon be staying with us had fled in the middle of the night, bringing nothing but the family jewels with them as they stole across the Mekong. "Family jewels" drew a chuckle from a few of the boys with dirtier minds. I wondered if the Mekong was very wide. How cold was the water? Had they rowed across? Swum? Secretly built a raft? They had then walked to a refugee camp in Thailand, where they had waited patiently for a Canadian visa. Some of the students wanted to know if they had come by boat, like the boat people we saw on the evening news. No, we were told. They had flown to Montreal. Others wanted to know if they had winter over there. The question excited Madame Nordet. "That's just it. They don't know what winter is like at all. They're from a part of the world where it's always warm. That's why we're rustling up tuques and mitts for the poor little darlings—they don't have any at all." That very evening, we all went through our homes with a fine-tooth comb to track down anything likely to protect a child's body from the cold and communism. The women of Saint-Ulric were instructed to begin knitting on the spot. The wool of a hundred sheep went into mitts, tuques, and scarves to protect the Laotians from the rigours of our winter. They would be living in a big white house by the river. The Mekong for the St. Lawrence. Was one body of water as good as another?

Apart from the Laotians, who were yet to arrive, otherness in our neck of the woods was limited to the sporadic presence of a handful of anglophones from New Brunswick or a few Indians on the Maria reserve. Plenty of families were called McNeil, Murray, or Robinson, but they all had Quebec roots, trunks, and leaves, like the maples in the gospels. They had long since forgotten Ireland and blended right in. Blending in. There was an art to blending in in Saint-Ulric and the other villages along the Gaspé Peninsula. I had learned that soon enough after coming to this school. Don't stand out. Say you like hockey. Don't be different. Madame Nordet showed us a photo of the Laotians who would soon be living among us. I took a good look. It wasn't going to be easy, I told myself silently.

And so it was that, one winter's day, a little Laotian girl joined our class. Almost every class in our little school took in a student from the large family. There were six of them in total. In normal circumstances, they would have gone to Toronto, Montreal, or Vancouver. They would never have taken Route 132 to find themselves in Saint-Ulric in the dead of a Quebec winter.

Before fleeing north, Mr. Vonvichit, as he was called, had been clerk of the court in Vientiane. So as not to condemn him to idleness, the immigration ministry had found a job for him at the Saint-Ulric peat bog. In a part of the country ravaged by unemployment, this had been enough to raise eyebrows. "A job? What about me? *I* don't have a job, do I?" Echoes of hushed conversations between parents reached me in the schoolyard. Mr. Vonvichit, whose job as clerk of the court in Laos had involved keeping the documents of the court in order, dealing with judges and lawyers, and wearing fancy shoes, now found himself gathering peat in a half-frozen field in eastern Quebec, behind the wheel of a monstrous machine that looked like a huge spider. Irony was not going to spare Mr. Vonvichit. Back in Laos, the Marxist revolutionaries had accused him of being too educated and sucking the blood of the proletariat. They had made his life impossible. When he left Vientiane with his wife and six children, he was about to be shipped off to a re-education camp, a place people generally didn't return from. In Canada, he was now driving a vacuum harvester. The Canadian government had managed to accomplish by peaceful means what the communists would have achieved through violence. Mr. Vonvichit was now a member of the Gaspé Peninsula's proletariat, envied for his stable, well-paid employment.

At school, Madame Nordet wrote the names of Mr. Vonvichit's six children on the blackboard. Phousavan,

Anousone, Khonesavanh, Paxathipatai, Nouphone, and Saravan. Our Laotians certainly broke up the monotony of Quebec's first names. We had to learn the names by heart before the family arrived. It was the least we could do. We were then asked to write the Vonvichit family's first names in our notebooks. We had to look up at the blackboard more than once to get them right. The names defied all logic and didn't even tell us the children's sex. The exercise quickly got out of hand. Within minutes, I could hear a couple of girls giggling. Not far from where I was sitting, a mischievous girl from Saint-Ulric had already come up with nicknames for our new friends. A few recesses later and the list of nicknames had done the rounds of the school. The eldest, Phousavan, was christened "Peasant Man," a name that was petty enough. Poor Anousone, set to join my sister's class, would be called "Anus One." Khonesavanh, the new girl in my class, was to be "Comment ça va?" And the unfortunate Paxathipatai was burdened with "Paxa Potato." Cute little Nouphone would be known to us as "New Phone," while little Saravan, still too young to go to school, would be— yes, you've guessed it—"Caravan." They hadn't yet set foot on Gaspé soil, and the Vonvichits had already been rechristened. But those among you who believe humour to be a backhanded compliment will be disappointed by the episode that followed. Khonesavanh walked into our classroom on a freezing winter day. Our new classmate had been in Canada for several weeks. She and her family had first been treated for a number of medical conditions.

Madame Nordet had told us that the Vonvichits came from a country where people sometimes carried diseases. "Sometimes they don't even know. They're not as lucky as you or I. And don't forget, they've never heard tell of Jesus. They're Buddhists. They believe in reincarnation."

One morning, the little Laotian girl came into the classroom with the principal. Madame Nordet asked her to stand in front of the class for everyone to get a good look at her. She didn't understand. For ten seconds, we watched her in deathly silence. She had big gentle eyes, long black hair, and smooth-looking skin. She stared at the floor and, after what to her must have seemed like three centuries, took her seat beside a girl by the name of Madone, to whom she had more or less been entrusted. Madone was to take Khonesavanh everywhere, introduce her to her friends, have her try out the swings, and protect her, all of which she managed admirably. She stepped in whenever she heard a lout call the new girl a "Chink," jeer "Comment ça va?", or spout forth other improprieties, letting the boor know in no uncertain terms that there would be consequences. Although the treatment dished out to the Laotians deeply saddened me, the attention focused on them spared me attacks by the other boys. Weeks went by without anyone hitting me. No one called me a faggot. The Laotians were attracting all the insults.

The week that Khonesavanh arrived coincided with a class skating trip to the arena in Matane. The poor little girl, terrorized by the huge frozen surface before her, teetered on a pair of old white skates and was dragged around the ice to whoops of joy. Two girls held her by the hand and tried to teach her in ten minutes what they had taken months to learn. Khonesavanh, her eyes wide, staggered across the ice like a puppet with its strings cut, Madone barely managing to keep her on her feet. Disaster was on its way, simply waiting for the right moment to befall us.

A couple of boys began to jostle the little girl, shouted "Comment ça va? Comment ça va?" Surprised, she let go of the hand that was holding her and toppled backward, smacking her head against the ice. A small crowd formed around her. She didn't move.

Beside the blue line on the ice, Madone held her in her arms, her eyes raised to heaven, desperately looking around for Madame Nordet or another adult. A scene of piety that still haunts me to this day.

She had to be taken to the hospital, where the doctors confirmed she had suffered a bad concussion. Madone wanted to die with shame. She blamed the incident on the old white skates, telling anyone who would listen that the blades were blunt, that they hadn't been sharpened properly. Buddhist or not, the little Laotian lived under the protective gaze of Madone, our very own Madonna.

Khonesavanh came back to school, mortified, a few days after the accident. The little Laotians stuck together for those first days among us. They closed off their circle to us, surrounded by noisy kids and risking no more than the odd glance outside the little world they had made for themselves. Sometimes an unflattering nickname would be heard rising out of the mass of students. The five brothers and sisters would tremble with fright, talk among themselves in Laotian, and avoid eye contact with us. The schoolchildren had been strictly forbidden from throwing snowballs, jostling the new arrivals, and *openly* making fun of them. One day, the smallest of the Laotian boys, who can't have been any older than eight, made an extraordinary discovery. As he watched one of his new Québécois schoolmates, he realized that the snow covering the schoolyard was malleable and could be made into balls that could be thrown, painting semi-circles across the sky. He bided his time. Then, one day when a little cretin shoved him, he threw his first snowball, whacking his assailant square on the forehead. From that moment on, the nicknames for the Laotians were virtually never heard again.

The young Vonvichits did not attend catechism class. They left the classroom in the morning to learn French with a teacher who had been taken on by the school board just for them. This lady had grown to love every one of the little refugees and spent many a happy hour teaching them French using pictures. "It's funny how there's money for that, but not for all the rest," another teacher had commented. Clearly, not everyone was in favour of the Laotians.

By virtue of the agreement with the government, the Vonvichit family spent four years in Saint-Ulric. When the four years were up, they disappeared. Other people moved into the house they'd been living in.

Mr. Vonvichit's job was given to a local, and Madone lost her little protégée. "Ungrateful" was the word on everyone's lips. "They got their citizenship and now they're off to the city! What else is new!" If you ask me, they took the most logical migration route, the same one I dreamed of taking myself every night. Sometimes I wonder whatever became of them. Whether, some winter nights, Khonesavanh's thoughts turn to Madone, who watched over her first days in Canada. I wonder if she learned to skate. I also wonder if they ever knew that their coming into my life had shown me there was another world out there, that another life was possible. I'm especially grateful to them for turning the Saint-Ulric welcoming committee's attention away from me, by their mere presence. For a few days at least, they had managed to find someone more different than I was.

Khonesavanh had come into our world just as we were feverishly preparing to receive the breath of the Holy Spirit. The first step of our preparations involved launching the miniature boat, a symbol for our Christian souls, out onto the St. Lawrence. The river that flowed into the ocean represented life. It had storms in store for us, but would also lead us on to brighter shores. Boats launched by students in previous years, we were told, had been found as far away as Newfoundland. The first and last names of all the confirmed were written on a piece of paper and rolled up in a canister that was tightly fastened to the boat, embarking on a voyage on the northern seas that would end up God knows where. A note was added to the list of names, encouraging anyone who might find the boat to throw it back into the sea and allow it to continue its journey among the currents, cod, seals, and glaciers. Madame Nordet showed us a letter from a couple of Newfoundlanders who were delighted to have found one of the boats. We had asked the English teacher to translate it for us. The Newfies assured us that they had returned the boat to the sea, letting it set sail for new ports. Launching the scale model was of the utmost importance to Madame Nordet. First, we had to come up with a name. The choice was to be put to a vote, in keeping with the rules of democracy. Each student was to suggest a name, then we'd all vote for our favourite. We were given a few days to think it over.

When the time came, I arrived at school convinced that my suggestion would win hands down. I had mulled it over all night. The name, in my view, had to reflect the northerly latitude where we lived, and evoke both the beauty of the north and the dreams of humanity, all while sounding suitably French. *The Aurore Boréale* seemed perfect. I had been tempted to suggest *The Aurora Borealis*, but I knew exactly how many punches that would earn me at the hands of the boys of Saint-Ulric. Madame Nordet wrote all the suggestions on the board. A list of improbable names appeared. *The Champion. The Dragon. The Sun. The Ulricois.* This final suggestion was put forward by a student by the name of Julie Santerre, who lived in a big house not far from us. She was a spoiled little blonde girl who owned all of Nathalie

Simard's records, a children's repertoire that had been slapped with an edict from the queen. Anne Boleyn deemed the singer's work too inane for our ears. Little Julie, as well as speaking with a forked tongue, came from a family of diehard federalists: they even went as far as flying the Canadian flag outside their home, which was just asking for it in the eyes of Henry VIII and Anne Boleyn. In the court, the intelligence of the family was regularly called into question. At school, the little girl was very popular with the others, thanks to her fashionable clothes and the toys that no one else had. Rumour had it that it took the Santerres up to two hours to unwrap all their Christmas gifts. Julie was also into figure skating, a sport that Anne Boleyn couldn't abide and that the king dismissed as boring and bourgeois. True, figure skaters reminded us that grace, agility, and vacuousness sometimes came in the same package. And so Julie suggested that our boat be called *The Ulricois*, a facile word she had no doubt arrived at by sticking together the words *Québécois* and *Saint-Ulric*. It was a ridiculous idea. All the others, mine included, were in with a shout. Why burden our boat with a name that no one would recognize? What would the Newfies say? The first round of voting confirmed my deepest fears. *The Ulricois* earned enough votes to make it into the second round. While *The Aurore Boréale* was eliminated straight away. Too many voters, I later learned, hadn't understood the name. Every girl in the class got behind Julie Santerre in the third round. Our boat would be called *The Ulricois*. I think that was the day when I first understood the fragility of democracy and just how pointless referendums can be. People rarely answer the question put in front of them. They vote for the little blonde girl in the mauve tutu twirling round and round on the ice. We applauded the winner, who smiled inanely, and placed the order with the carpenter tasked with building the little boat.

In the meantime, we had to brush up on the gospels and the Acts of the Apostles. Madame Nordet invited the local priest in Saint-Ulric into our classroom, the first member of the clergy to put in an appearance so far. Our teacher told us three days ahead of time that he was coming. Before even sitting down, the surly man demanded that the little Laotian girl be banished on the spot.

"Get that one out of here!"

"Oh, yes! I had forgotten, Father."

The little Asian girl was politely accompanied to the library.

"Those people aren't Catholic," he said. "They're *Buddhist*."

He said "Buddhist" the way you might have said "Soviet intercontinental ballistic missile" back then. "Buddhist" was the magic word that had you excused from the whole rigmarole. The priest had about as much personality as a dead rat. I suddenly felt the urge to say I was a Buddhist, too, but I thought of the beautiful hymn we were about to launch into and decided to keep any thoughts of conversion to myself. They didn't much go in for ecumenical dialogue in Saint-Ulric. Once the outsider had been taken away, the baptized among us discussed the Holy Spirit's impending arrival. The priest, an old fellow on the cusp of retirement, didn't muster much excitement for the whole affair. He often grew impatient, raised his eyes heavenward after every question, and kept glancing at his watch. Madame Nordet stood there swooning, smiling at the priest's every word.

A tall, skinny kid whispered to his neighbour, grinning while the priest went on about the Pentecost. It was no great surprise to anyone who knew him. He was one of the Desrosiers, a family of farmers who lived just up from us on the east side of Route Athanase, the road that marked the official border between the municipalities of Matane and Saint-Ulric. It separated the parishes, too. The Desrosiers, who straddled both kingdoms, went to our school all the same, because they could take the school bus and because they felt more of an affinity with Saint-Ulric. The Desrosiers family, which was viewed with suspicion by the teachers because of its offspring's disappointing school performances, also went to the village church. Irked by the interruption, the priest stopped talking and looked the unfortunate boy square in the eye.

"Are you ever going to stop talking? Would you like to continue in my place?"

The boy reddened.

"I don't even know why they let you come here. You're not even from my parish!"

Alain Desrosiers stared hard at the floor.

Madame Nordet didn't know what to do with herself. The priest brought his interminable presentation to an end, blessed us half-heartedly, and walked back to the presbytery. I secretly thanked the king for building his house west of the road. It's so easy to inadvertently find yourself on the wrong side of an argument.

The school year slowly drifted past, and the winkle still hadn't burst in on my spiritual life. I tried to reach out to the Laotians. Their manners and courtesy were unparalleled in our village. The eldest boy, Phousavan, was becoming more popular with the girls at school. They would ask him to write their names in the snow using the Laotian alphabet. The exercise seemed to charm them. One day, a girl broached the subject of whether the Laotians' presence was useful, or indeed desirable, in our village. At least, I think that's what she meant when she said, "What're they all doing here any-ways?" I was at a loss for an answer.

I lost touch with the Laotians and I've never met any others. None that I know of, at any rate. Not so long ago, I happened to read in an article published by a university in Montreal that Phousavan Vonvichit was conducting some very complex medical research. Something to do with HIV. I'm not quite sure what. If ever I bump into him, I'll ask him to do something I never dared ask in Saint-Ulric: to write my name in the snow using the Laotian alphabet. It snows in Montreal, too.

That year, it was decreed that the students at our school, École Monseigneur-Belzile, would put on a

125

talent show for their parents' entertainment. Skits, songs, acrobatics, a piano recital—every ounce of the school's talent was to be distilled for all to see on a small wooden stage that was opened out in the gym for the occasion. Preparations for the talent show and our confirmation took precedence over grammar, math, and geography. You didn't need to excel at geography at our school at any rate. Knowing which parish you belonged to was quite sufficient. We worked feverishly on our comedy routines and a song or two. Rumour had it the Laotians had something up their sleeves, too. A dance number. We would have to wait and see.

On the evening of the talent show, parents filled the theatre-for-a-night to catch their kids' performances. Fathers, mothers, grandparents, uncles, and aunts piled into the gym, listening to the wind whistle through the freezing night air as they waited for the show to begin. No one had yet set eyes on the Laotians' number. The show got underway. First, the audience was treated to a hilarious monologue from a young boy dressed in a white soutane. He played a young priest, all at sea since Vatican II had decreed that mass was now to be said in French, and had mistranslated the Latin *petere* (to pray) as *péter* (to fart). He urged his parishioners to let flatulence solve the problems of their existence. *"Péter tous les jours pour que Dieu vous entende!"* he shouted. "Let rip every day and God will hear you!" The audience fell over themselves laughing. Bodily functions are always good for a laugh. Next came acrobatics. Human pyramids, jumps, and contortion acts. The crowd went wild as a boy walked across the stage on his hands. Then, a musical number. A little girl with the voice of an angel sang Mireille Mathieu's *Santa Maria de la mer*, the touching lyrics familiar to everyone… "Santa Mariiiiiaaaa!" A lady wiped away a tear from her eye.

The Laotian girls' performance was finally announced midway through the show. A murmur made its way from one side of the room to the other. The Vonvichit family's three oldest daughters took their place on stage in the darkness. We still couldn't see them. Then the spotlight fell on the dancers. They were dressed in traditional Laotian costumes. The audience gasped in admiration. Anousone, Khonesavanh, and Nouphone were wearing long embroidered dresses with delicate details and stitching. The silk, scattered with sequins and gold decorations, reflected the white light. Their hands clasped before their chests as though in prayer, the Laotians waited for their musical accompaniment to begin. For the first time, we saw them all made-up like the Thai dancers you see in tourism brochures. But most remarkable of all wasn't their dresses or their light sandals, it was the golden three-pointed hats that stood straight upon their heads, making them each twenty centimetres taller. I had never seen anything so beautiful, so delicate. The music began. We didn't understand the choreography at first. The three girls were all lined up, facing the audience, and didn't seem to be moving. Then suddenly we realized their hands had shifted without us noticing. Their wrists performed movements with surgical precision. Not since Nadia Comaneci had I seen such grace and beauty. Did communism make people more graceful? The idea seemed to have some merit. I was so busy trying to figure out how they were managing to change position without me noticing that it took me a while to see that their feet were also moving, just as imperceptibly. Nouphone, the youngest, was advancing to the front of the stage while the others glided back. But it was impossible to see what was going on until the movement had already been completed. The dance lasted around five minutes, during which time the Laotians moved to the front and back of the stage as though they had tiny wheels on their feet. The captivated audience was aware it was witnessing a scene that bordered on the supernatural. Some of the boys began to imagine the Laotian girls had magical powers, that none of it was possible, that it was all some sort of trick. The number was over. The applause built slowly and quickened as the audience emerged from the spell. Mrs. Vonvichit seemed content. The Laotians disappeared backstage.

I think that the people of Saint-Ulric left the school that evening pondering questions they would never have considered before the show. For my part, I filed the Laotian dance away in a corner of my mind reserved for things that evoke wonder without being entirely comprehensible. Like Pentecost, the feeding of the multitudes, and the migration of the snow goose. When I walked out into the freezing Gaspé night, the aurora borealis were flickering on the horizon. They were the same colour as the Laotian girls' costumes and they, too, moved back and forth without me being able to grasp exactly how.

Our boat was to set sail a few days later. The ice on the St. Lawrence had melted, the blues of the sea were once again starting to merge with those of the sky. The birds were back from Virginia, Jacques Brel was singing *La Fanette*, and it was high time for a boat to be put to sea. When the day came, the whole class set out for the stretch of beach that was to be used to launch *The Ulricois*. Deep down I hoped the boat would sink after a second or two, leaving no one in any doubt that a boat that was supposed to represent my soul should never have been given a name like that. Standing on the shore, we sang *Come Holy Spirit* for the millionth time. The school had recruited a local fisherman to tow the boat out to sea.

The tide was at its highest. Clumps of green seaweed flung in by the waves washed over the shingle beach and up to our feet. A hundred metres away, a crazy young guy on a moped played chicken with the waves, zigzagging his way across the foreshore. He came to a sudden stop before a huge pile of seaweed that had just rolled in front of him. Without it being clear why, he clambered off his bike and bent down over the seaweed. He poked at it with his foot and shrieked in horror. He jumped back onto his moped and sped up toward the road. The incident had no effect on our singing, but I watched it unfold out of the corner of my eye. We sang as we walked back, our hearts filled with hope that *The Ulricois* might be fished out of the water in Newfoundland or maybe even the French islands of Saint-Pierre and Miquelon.

At suppertime back in the court of Henry VIII, I announced that *The Ulricois* had been put to sea to the east and that it was carrying my soul off to new lands. The king and queen considered the whole undertaking a childish and slightly idiotic Catholic fancy, never suspecting that this departure, in fact, heralded my destiny. The king had much more entertaining things to talk about. He had spent a tiring day answering calls for help that were much more pressing than the imminent visit of the Holy Spirit. Between two mouthfuls of potatoes, he explained that a distraught mother had called the police after her son had come home from the beach in tears. A dead body had rolled in front of his moped while he was riding along the sand. Henry VIII had headed over to discover a pile of seaweed wrapped around the still-frozen body of a sailor from the *Hudson Transport*. It must have been one of the panic-stricken sailors who had fallen into the water when their lifeboat overturned. The king had picked up the body that had been biding its time all winter long beneath the frozen St. Lawrence. The body, he explained, had been very well preserved and the man's flesh had not yet begun to decay. The *Hudson Transport* sailors were Russian, he said, which was news to me. Apparently the freezing water and sub-zero temperatures had preserved the sailor's features perfectly. He was a young man, his eyes still open, when the king had arrived. Or rather, just one of his eyes had been open. The other was missing. A winkle had taken the place of the left eye of that Russian sailor who had died of cold over Christmas just off Saint-Ulric.

Forks clattered down onto plates. The graphic image of a drowned man flashed before my eyes. In that instant, I resolved to do two things: First, to go to Russia one day. And second, to never eat another winkle.

The ceremony was held for our solemn confirmation. We formed two neat lines and waited for the Holy Spirit, which had taken the form of the archbishop of Rimouski. It was my one and only encounter with the Holy Spirit. I haven't seen it since. Or the Laotians. I don't know which I miss most. The strange thing is that the miracle of Pentecost, with its tongues of fire imparting wisdom and knowledge, had only the slightest of effects on the children in my class. The day I started grade four in Saint-Ulric, at the age of ten, there were fourteen boys in the class. Four years later, in grade eight, there were only two of us left. The others had dropped out of school, much to the despair of Madame Nordet, who had given her all.

# CHAPTER 4

# The Dog (1980)

ON CERTAIN MISTY MAY EVENINGS, a stray mongrel dog can be seen wandering around the port in Matane. She has haunted the wharves since 1981, when hulking Soviet ships would cast anchor there, come to stock up on wood from our forests to take back to Russia. No one knows where the dog came from. One day, she must have left one of the ships to go for a walk and been late getting back. She has wandered there ever since, exposed to the raging winds. At twilight, she comes barking out of the fog, walks over to you, and sits up and begs, waiting for a treat. She does everything she can to show off just how intelligent she is, just how many tricks she has learned. If, one evening in May, you should happen to find yourself shivering on the wharf after some sad event or other has left you doubting all possibility of a future, simply wait a while, and the little dog will come trotting out of the fog. She'll come straight up to you; she's not shy. You'll have planned ahead and brought meatballs to give her as a treat when she stands up on her hind legs and turns around three times, barking all the while. She's just adorable. You can't help but love her.

But the dog hasn't always lived on the Gaspé Peninsula. There was a time, back in the 1950s, when she roamed the freezing streets of Moscow with her mother and brothers and sisters. Even though she's clearly a mongrel, you might be able to guess at her pedigree. There's surely some husky, a little spitz, and a lot of terrier in her. And, as is usually the case for mongrels, you'd have a hard time finding her mother. She won't talk about her either. She wasn't trained to think of her mother; she was trained for much greater missions. So, at first, you'll say to yourself, "Oh look, a little dog on this dreary Gaspé wharf. How cute! How reassuring! I'll play with her a while and put the fright behind me. This place gives me the creeps!" And how right you'll be.

She'll disappear by dawn, the way she came, back into the mist. You'll still hear her barking on the wharf at sunrise. Like a cry for help. I once told a Toronto psychiatrist the story of the little ghost dog in the port of Matane. Since he enjoyed the story and took lots of notes on his pad as he listened, let me tell it again so you, too, can enjoy it.

You can take out your notepads.

If, one Saturday afternoon in summer, after your trip to Matane, you happen to find yourself at the national archives and you take the time to read the microfilm for the local newspaper, *La Voix gaspésienne*, you'll see that January 1981 was "Soviet Month" in our little port. It was also in 1981 that, thanks to a Romanian stamp, I almost became the first cosmonaut from Canada. Or Quebec. I wasn't entirely sure because in the spring of 1980, there had been a referendum campaign in Quebec. Quebecers were asked a very long and very complicated question to which they were to answer yes or no. If I remember correctly, they wanted to know if, possibly, and in consideration of certain conditions—all somewhat uncertain and enigmatic—Quebecers felt vaguely inclined to envisage talks on the beginning of negotiations leading to the drawing-up of a plan (or process) with a view to national affirmation. All completely out of context, naturally. The answer to the question was short and laconic. Quebecers, women especially, rejected the proposal. I had known, ever since the vote on the name for *The Ulricois*, that the whole thing was doomed to fail. People rarely answer the question they're asked. They tend to still be considering the last one. Or else they say what they're told to or what the figure skater said. That way they can always blame her when the time of reckoning rolls around.

The adjective that best describes the king and queen's state of mind throughout this period would perhaps be "frenetic." There was no mystery about how they felt, as witnessed by the two Félix Leclerc records that played in the Saint-Ulric home until the walls themselves began to sing along to the sad songs of our national poet. A clear tendency emerged from their remarks on the situation: opponents of Quebec sovereignty were lacking in intelligence. *The Nos Don't Know. Yes is Best*. That just about summed up all we needed to wrap our heads around in May 1980. The challenge was explaining it to those who just didn't get it. The queen had decided to opt for visual aids to achieve this pedagogical objective, returning from Matane one day with little badges sporting the Parti québécois logo in her bag. There were three types. The first was a simple round photograph of a smiling René Lévesque. René Lévesque was, they explained, an intelligent and cultured man who wanted all Quebecers to one day become equally intelligent and cultured. The second was a simple white YES on a blue background with a little fleur-de-lys (so that it was clear what you were saying yes to). The third required a certain appreciation of stylistic device. Against a white background, there was an oval-shaped Canadian flag cracked in half. A little blue bird, more or less shaped like the fleur-de-lys, was flying out of the egg. This liberating image appealed to me right away. My sister and I decided we would wear the badges to school. This seemed to please the queen. The things we agree to in return for a smile! To dispel any doubts as to where his political allegiances lay, Henry VIII managed to find a three-metre by four-metre poster somewhere. A huge YES on a blue background. He nailed it to the house. I think it could be seen from the moon.

One morning in the spring of 1980, we were waiting for the school bus. My sister was wearing René Lévesque's face, while I proudly sported the cracked egg. This wasn't the first time we had indulged in such eccentric behaviour. The bus arrived and we got on. Usually I was greeted with an affectionate "homo!" or "faggot!" but that morning no one looked at me. All eyes were on our house and the gigantic YES. A deathly silence fell over the bus for several seconds, then the murmuring started. The bus driver, a crusty old man, roared at us to sit down. He had a small maple leaf pinned to his cap. I began to suspect our behaviour might not be entirely appropriate.

At school I realized that our political initiative left no one indifferent. The teachers gave us funny looks. Some of them whispered to each other when I walked by. The next day, dozens of children came to school wearing NO badges. Some poor little girl had been given a photo of Pierre Elliott Trudeau to wear. The children formed a circle around her, asking who the scrawny old man was. Pierre Elliott Trudeau was, she explained, an intelligent and cultured man who wanted Quebecers to remain Canadian. The little girl noted with pride that he was the prime minister of Canada. "How can he be intelligent if he's voting no?" I reasoned. She had no answer. Then she went to complain to Madame Nordet, who told me to say I was sorry for questioning the prime minister's intelligence. "I'm sorry he's stupid," I replied, thinking myself very spiritual. There ensued a lecture on the respect due to the prime minister of Canada and the virtues of federalism. By way of punishment, Madame Nordet set me three pages of math for the following day. Adding fractions as punishment for the crime of *lèse-majesté*.

René Lévesque and Pierre Elliott Trudeau, by virtue of their age and the way they behaved, seemed to belong to another species altogether, if you asked us. They were part of the tribe of grey, wrinkled people who were never at a loss for words. A little like Madame Nordet. Although Madame Nordet was fond of Mr. Trudeau. I had figured that out after the pillowcase incident. In the spring of 1980, she had decided to teach us embroidery. For our first exercise, we had to embroider a pattern along the edge of a white pillowcase. We were to trace the pattern with a lead pencil and get Madame Nordet's approval before we started embroidering. I found the whole thing immensely tiresome. And the queen was on my side. "Embroidery? What use is that? Can't she teach you more math instead?" Anne Boleyn liked math. She liked it as much as Madame Nordet sometimes hated it. Madame Nordet liked embroidery, catechism, and Pierre Elliott Trudeau. As for me, I had traced three little fleurs-de-lys in pencil and was getting ready to embroider them in blue thread. I showed my design to Madame Nordet, who reacted as though I had showed her an erect penis.

"You're going to embroider *that*?"

"Yes."

She took the blue thread out of her drawer and slammed it down on her desk.

"Here!"

Little Julie Santerre, witness to the scene, hurriedly erased her work and drew a bunch of maple leaves on her pillowcase instead. She had no problems getting her hands on the red thread and all the help from Madame Nordet she needed. I got by as best I could in my corner with my fleurs-de-lys. I was almost happy for Julie Santerre. One day, a teacher had asked her to point to Canada on a map of the world. She had been unable to find the huge pink stain covering almost a quarter of the northern hemisphere. She had stood there, stunned, in front of the map, swaying back and forth before the dumbfounded teacher like a little idiot. Julie had let slip a shrill little laugh. The teacher had smiled and sent her back to her desk.

There was something reassuring in the way Julie Santerre was so fond of something she didn't know the first thing about. I think it's called "faith." Madame Nordet taught us our country was so big that a train leaving Halifax would take five days to reach Vancouver. One of the children asked her if she'd ever been to Halifax. She said no. Then he asked if she had ever been to Vancouver. She hadn't either, but just knowing that Pierre Elliott Trudeau had been was enough for her to like the place.

In the schoolyard, the badge war was raging. The reds on one side, the blues on the other. Believe it or not, a few kids even improvised comedy sketches using the faces of René Lévesque and Pierre Elliott Trudeau. They came up with all kinds of hilarious conversations, turning the badges into puppets. Come to think of it, I think their little dramas were more worthwhile and more intelligent than anything else said about the political situation back then. I was pleased to see the clash, in a way. I did well out of it. Before the referendum campaign, I didn't understand why I would be thrown to the asphalt, threatened with death, and showered with abuse. I suffered for naught. My pain served no cause. My sister explained to me that it was because of the king. And it was true that, fairly regularly, Henry VIII would arrest petty thieves and dole out fines to my classmates' parents. My school could boast of being home to an effective, if modest, mafia. It goes without saying that I paid dearly for the king's overzealousness, but the sovereignty referendum gave a political dimension to my martyrdom. For once, I was being hit for an idea, a dream. The very worst insults slid off my separatist shell like water off a duck's back. Thanks to the Parti québécois, my suffering had meaning at last.

The referendum passed. The badges disappeared. The huge white YES on our house was taken to the basement and perhaps even burned. The list of hammer words grew longer. Now it included "sovereignty," "referendum," "Pierre Elliott Trudeau," and "the Yvettes." Of the latter,

I still have a vague memory of French-Canadian women dressed in long peasant skirts and singing *Un Canadien errant*. They were proud to serve their families, their husbands, their land. They had voted no. They gave themselves the name "Yvette" and fought the new ideas that were shaking kitchen walls across Quebec. The Yvettes had managed to guarantee that every last child would experience the Canadian childhoods they had known. The Yvettes were the polar opposite of Anne Boleyn, who had also had a Canadian childhood. People say the referendum was lost because of the Yvettes—or that it was won thanks to them, depending on your point of view. I don't know anymore. One thing I do know, because you have to know some things, after all, is that Anne Boleyn was a math whiz.

But maybe math isn't your thing. Since you're still reading this, you're probably more into mysterious, exotic stories. Out of curiosity, you'll go back down to the wharf in Matane for a second evening to wait for the adorable little dog you took such a liking to. She'll be over the moon to see you again. She'll show you everything she's learned all over again. Then, she'll sit by the edge of the wharf, a little tired from the effort. You'll sit down beside her. She'll look out to sea—a sea as black as the cosmos—then up at the stars through the fog. She'll bark three times at the light blinking on a Boeing, and begin to whine softly. You'll stroke her head to calm her. Her fur will be a little curly to the touch. Tenderly, you'll think out loud, "Hey, I'm going to call you Little

Curly. It suits you." Then something extraordinary will happen. The little dog will begin to talk, in a Russian accent. A talking dog is surprising enough. But a dog that talks in a Russian accent is astonishing. She'll roll her r's. Once you get over your astonishment, you'll gather your wits and find her accent perfectly charming. "It's funny you say that," she'll say. "Little Curly was my first name. Before that, I didn't have one. Oleg gave me my first name. *Kudryavka*. It means "little curls" or "a little curly" in Russian. When he found me, I was running around the streets of Moscow in the middle of October. The nights were freezing already. A little like here, only over there I was with my mom. We combed the streets for something to eat. That's all we knew how to do. Beg. We weren't the sharpest tools in the shed. It's strange. I miss all that tonight." You'll stare out at the shadowy Gulf of St. Lawrence with her, thinking that this little dog, which seemed so cheerful ten minutes ago, is actually rather sad.

You won't dare say a word.

The royal edicts of 1977 banned stupidity from the royal court. You had to have your wits about you. And so the queen came up with an admirable program for training grey matter. "You need to be able to count," she said. So we played cards and Monopoly. "You also need to be able to write." Long games of Scrabble and other word games were organized. I enjoyed them all. They filled the gulf that the little earthquakes had opened up between me and the queen. But prudence was key: board games were not beyond censure, and the list of hammer words was strictly enforced. If, for instance, I wound up with all the letters spelling D-I-V-O-R-C-E on my little wooden rack, letting me use up all my tiles at once for fifty bonus points, I would have to decide against it and opt for a shorter word instead. This rule made the games more interesting. It was when she was turning something over in her mind, counting, or thinking that the queen seemed to be happiest. I never saw her more satisfied than when one of us spelled out a tricky word on the table. She reacted admirably well to signs of intelligence. The sullen look she wore whenever the king was drinking would lift for a few minutes, giving way to an expression that was full of admiration. One day, two years after the referendum, she gave me a Rubik's cube as a present and an article cut out of a science magazine that explained how to solve the puzzle. The article was incredibly complicated. I had to, for example, memorize dozens of formulas like GHD'HGHDG'. But I made such an effort that I was soon able to complete the cube in just one minute and nine seconds. She also gave me a short novel called *Wargames*, which she asked me to translate into French. My awkward translation of the title was *La guerre est un jeu* (War is a game), which seemed plausible at the time. I tripped over every other word, not making it beyond the third page. It was a story about spies and Russian missiles. The world was going to be wiped out by Soviet nuclear bombs. It gave me nightmares. Every time I met one of the queen's challenges, I got the otherwise improbable in return: a sign of affection in the form of a compliment. For *Wargames*, she let me know that I had disappointed her, that she had thought me more intelligent than that. Translation can sometimes be the way to a lady's heart.

One day, disaster struck. Madame Nordet was very, very ill for a whole month. A woman from Matane came to fill in for her. Unlike Madame Nordet, the substitute loved teaching math and followed the new provincial programs to the letter. As ill luck would have it, she also had to test our math skills for a school report card. She gave me seventy-five percent, a score of apocalyptic proportions and a far cry from my usual average. And the bad news didn't stop there. My sister's grade 6 teacher also decided to put the screws to her students, meaning that she ended up with a score comparable to my own. We smelled a conspiracy. And there probably was one. In the 1970s, the Quebec government realized that younger Quebecers were hopeless at math. Which is what happens when you leave a people's education in the hands of the Church. And so Quebec's pen-pushers put dozens of math whizzes in charge of coming up with a program designed to turn us all into little Descartes. Textbooks were printed, teachers trained. Well, most teachers. School timetables were filled up with math classes. In less than fifteen years, Quebec schoolchildren became math champions. Even today, when you compare the math skills of students around the world, Quebecers rank third behind the Chinese of Hong Kong and the Koreans. That's really something.

My sister and I got our report cards on the same day. We had to get them signed. I remember us sitting in the bus like two condemned prisoners on a tumbril, on our way to the gallows. The bus slowly climbed the country roads, across the snowy fields. Stomach cramps. Sobbing from my sister. We were bringing irrefutable proof of our insignificance and stupidity back to the castle, stamped with the seal of the Matane school board. Certified morons. In ten minutes, the king and queen would know the pathetic condition our brains were in. We were unworthy of the court, and no Rubik's cube was going to change their minds. The queen's wrath was terrible. The king's was even worse. Echoes of their conversation reached me in my chambers. They were deliberating the sentence. We were called in. They were both sitting on their thrones, sceptre and shield in hand. The image did not bode well. The verdict was returned.

*In the case of the unsatisfactory mathematics grade, the Crown has decided the accused shall be found guilty of apathy and stupidity, crimes that in this court shall never be tolerated. The Crown has decided the sentence must set an example for such an unspeakable misdemeanour. The accused shall therefore be condemned to spend one half-hour every evening before an open mathematics text-book and shall solve algebraic equations until such time as their little heads finally agree to let in the light. You must understand that the Kingdom will soon no longer be in a position to support you, that you must fly with your own wings. The only means of achieving this is to be*

*the best, and that includes in mathematics. Yes, you shall*
*go far, very far, but for that you will have to be strong in*
*mathematics. Otherwise a life of poverty and destitution*
*awaits. Do I make myself clear? After doing the dishes,*
*you will go downstairs to your chambers and throw your-*
*selves into said equations. The sentence begins at this very*
*instant. The King has spoken. Now disappear before we*
*change our minds.*

We would go far. So they had seen right through my
plan. The plan to go very far from Saint-Ulric, Matane,
and the king and queen. They might have guessed the
goal, but I think they misunderstood how I was going
to go about it. In my mind, math would be useful only
in helping me figure out how many kilometres I could
put between me and them. My sister was given a heavier
sentence than mine. For some reason, the king decided,
in concert with the queen, that she was to cease all
experiments with makeup, effective immediately. Such
vulgar paintwork was setting her on a downward path;
her future did not look bright. The findings were con-
clusive: the application of cosmetics to skin abruptly
halted all powers of mathematical reasoning. I was to
set my translations and Rubik's cube to one side to concentrate on factors and percentages.

It is worth mentioning, with regard to this story,
that the king and queen occupied different functions.
The king was outraged, there was no doubt, but it was
the queen who took corrective action. The order was
given by one throne and executed by the other. And it

didn't take us long to realize that the king was hope-less at math. He couldn't figure out the answers, grew impatient, and began to swear. It was all the nuns' fault. They hadn't taught him a thing. The queen, on the other hand, performed each step of every equation clearly and rationally. It was all thanks to the nuns. They had taught her everything she knew. Her talent was prodigious. Give her what looked to be an impossible problem and, after a few seconds of hard thinking, she would show us how to solve it with disarming ease. The exercises plunged her into a state of ecstasy that we seldom asso-ciated with her. I think it was the queen who taught me you could get neurons drunk. With Anne Boleyn, math suddenly became clear. It had no truck with sentimen-tality. It never made a maple tree out of a sycamore, any more than it turned water into wine. Math reassured me and patched up the multiple cracks that had fractured my relationship with the queen.

My sentence paid off. I got 100% in math on my next report card. My sister continued to put on makeup in secret.

If the little dog's early revelations haven't saddened you to the point of losing heart in the story, you'll want to stay close to her because you'll sense she's in the mood for a chat. And it isn't every day that you meet a Russian-accented dog in the port of Matane, or even in the port of Amsterdam, for that matter. Her story will have intrigued you. But whoever is this Oleg character? "Oleg? He was my owner. Oleg Gazenko. A

147

real good-looking gentleman. He lured me over with some leftover stew. When he put me in his car, there were already two other little dogs in there. Albina and Muchka. Poor Oleg! He took us to a very strange and very well-heated place. He fed us often, but we had to earn our meals. He had us sit, lie down, get back up, and run around. Albina and Muchka were slower on the uptake. It wasn't that they weren't capable of learning; they just didn't want to, that's all. They might have been only too happy to accept Oleg's meatballs, but they didn't trust him at all. Things took a turn for the worse when the real training began. Oleg put us in narrow metal boxes. No longer than we were. Then he banged against the sides, making as much noise as he could with a hammer. The game was to not fly into a panic. To learn how to stay calm. I wriggled every which way at the start. You see, I was used to walking wherever I pleased through the streets of the capital, as free as could be. And now, dear old Oleg was shutting me away in a metal box. Then one day, I understood that I had as much influence on Oleg as he had on me. All I had to do was give in to his whims and he would feed me. We dogs, you know, we'll do just about anything for food. We'd walk for miles and miles. Not only did he feed me, he began to be very nice to me. He would stroke me. Well done, *Kudryavka*, he'd say. And he looked so happy. He wore an ecstatic expression that I didn't understand. Was that really all he wanted? Albina and Muchka still hadn't understood. They kept on panicking, barking their heads off, biting, scratching. Oleg kept us in the little boxes for days. Then one day he spun us around very quickly in a machine. I couldn't move. I was stuck to the side of the box. We turned round and round like that for hours. I got sick. Oleg looked so worried when he picked me up. I think he thought I was dead. *Limonchik*, are you OK? he asked softly. He also called me *Limonchik*. Little lemon. Poor Oleg. Albina and Muchka were close to death. Muchka was sick for days. I think they didn't like being shut away like that. Have you ever been shut away? Has someone ever put you in a box no longer than your body for days and days?" You won't answer the question. Even if you have been shut away in a tight space for days and days, you won't speak. Not so much out of respect for Kudryavka's tragic story, but because, let's be honest, it's not so easy bringing that kind of thing to the surface. And it was all such a long time ago... Why bring such ugliness to mind when the world has so much beauty to rejoice in? Perhaps you'll want to adopt the little dog. For her to be yours forever. She'll say no. "I can't follow you," she'll say, in her lovely Russian accent. "You're perfectly nice, and pleasant company, too, but I am condemned to wander this dreary non-place in the dark and cold. But I do know that one day one of the huge cargo ships from my country will come back for me. Maybe the *Pavel Ponomarev* or the *Nina Kukoverova*. It doesn't matter which. They'll come back for me. They've forgotten me, that's all. I can't leave here. They'll pick me up, you'll see, and take me to Murmansk. From there, I'll hop on a truck heading to Moscow and be reunited with my mom and sisters. Ah! Just wait till they hear my story! Do you have another meatball for the trip?"

You will have thought of everything.

Meat. In the house in Saint-Ulric, supper was often masticated in poisonous silence. To relieve the tension, the king would tell us all about his day in the service of the state. What stories he had! Little does the tourist travelling the Gaspé Peninsula in his camper van suspect that the region is a hive of little tragedies and family dramas, that in these sleepy parts, crimes of passion echo louder than in cities. Sometimes, while I slowly sipped my soup, plotting my escape from the kingdom, he would tell his stories. A boy my sister's age had killed himself one village over in Baie-des-Sables. That was the best thing about having a police officer for a father: you would hear some piece of news at school and that night at supper, you would get the full eyewitness account. Because we already knew all about it. Sister Monique of the Passion, a math teacher at École Monseigneur-Belzile, had already told us, urging us to pray for the poor child's soul. It was, it seemed, an affair of the heart. A girl had made fun of him. That seemed weak to me. That same evening, the king came home from work sad. He had been called to the parents' house to go through the usual formalities. I've never understood why people call the police at times like that. Between the soup and the mashed potatoes, he told us the boy had used a 12-gauge shotgun, which seemed to be a very bad thing indeed. According to Henry VIII, this particular type of weapon hurls bullets in every direction to annihilate its target. A weapon like that doesn't leave a neat little red dot in the centre of the forehead like you see in the movies. When placed in the mouth, it rips off half your head and leaves chunks of it lying everywhere. And that's what the king found that day. A thirteen-year-old brain plastered across the ceiling and over the walls. The sound of people struggling to swallow could be heard around the table. The queen gave the king a reproachful look. Not in front of the little brother. On other nights, we would hear about a hairdresser in Sainte-Félicité who hanged herself after breaking up with her boyfriend. A spate of suicides. Not the kind of things you read about on postcards of pretty sunsets. A life lesson usually followed. "Come see me before you do anything so stupid." I didn't get it. The king and queen would have been the last people I would ever have turned to. Fortunately, I didn't feel much like hanging myself yet. That would come. I hadn't yet discovered the reassuring efficacy of sleeping pills.

Some days, I think that if the Sûreté du Québec were to take a photo of every suicide victim on the Gaspé Peninsula and send it to a member of the House of Commons in Ottawa, then things might change. Maybe then would come the change Pierre Elliott Trudeau had promised when he raised his voice to convince Quebecers to remain Canadian.

But we don't bother MPs with that type of thing. Instead, we send them invitations to go salmon fishing, climb Mont Albert, go heli-skiing, or take a photo of Percé Rock, even if that often involves waiting for the fishermen to take down the body of the man who's just hanged himself in the hole in the rock. We usually get them to come see us in the summer; the roads are better then.

Then, there was also the gloomy procession of accident victims whose limbs, after flying off at all angles across the badly kept roads of the Gaspé Peninsula, would land with a thud on our dinner table. A head with its skull split open was still rolling around in a corner somewhere. It belonged—irony of ironies—to the head of the Matane police force, who had been run over by a truck on his way to work one day. Other nights, it was a liquored-up husband who had beaten his wife so hard with I don't know what that the neighbours had called the police to put a stop to the racket. When he arrived on the scene, my father would find a woman covered in bruises defending her husband from the police. The raving lunatic would be hauled away under the children's reproachful gaze. "Where are you taking our dad? Who's going to rape us every evening now?" In a ramshackle village in the backcountry, an old pervert was trading smokes for blowjobs from twelve-year-olds. There were also stories of drug trafficking by biker gangs, break-ins, and countless violations of the Highway Code. The king's days were nothing but a depressing succession

152

of fines, dead bodies, crime, violence, calls for help, and hard times. When he returned to his castle, he must have thought our family frustrations more than a little pointless.

Supper in Saint-Ulric invariably ended with an order from the king or queen. "The dishes." Staring out at the forest from the kitchen window, my hands in warm soapy water, I wondered who would help my sister do the dishes if I blasted my brains out all over the ceiling. I wasn't cruel enough to leave my chores to her. "You can dry, Sis! And make sure you wipe off all the sauce stains. Otherwise Anne Boleyn will shout at us again." Just behind us we could hear the wet sounds of the sovereigns kissing. Their bellies full, they rubbed their moist snouts together. It turned my stomach in the most indescribable way. Nausea.

Should you return for a third evening to the wharf in Matane, this time you'll have thought to bring double meatball rations. The little dog will have suddenly stopped talking the previous night. Impossible to get another word out of her. She'll have fallen silent right after her heart-rending story about the centrifuge. She'll have thrown up a few meatballs and disappeared back into the thick fog down by the wharf in Matane. You'll be curious, eager to hear how the story ends. You'll whistle to her. "Kudryavka! Kudryavka! Are you there?" She might not come. You'll try to call her Limonchik. Her name will reverberate three times around the deserted port. Because there's not a lot going on there nowadays.

The heyday of Russian cargo ships has been and gone. They're rusting away somewhere on a beach in Cuba or Angola. You might find the whole thing most disturbing. Perhaps you'll want to call the Humane Society. You'll be just about to head back when, against all odds, you'll hear Limonchik barking. She'll run over to you. You'll go misty-eyed you'll be so happy to see her. She'll give you a real warm welcome, run around you three times, jumping up and barking. Because, whenever she's not talking, the little stray barks. She's a little barker. Or *Laika*, as they say in Russian. She'll wolf down the meatballs you brought and even the dog biscuit. For an instant, you'll feel as though you've found a friend. Man's best friend, ready to lay down her life for him. "So, Limonchik? Still talking? Would you like to tell me more about your lovely trip to Russia? Did you go to Saint Petersburg? Vladivostok? Did you take the train with Oleg Gazenko?" At the sound of Oleg Gazenko's name, the little dog will stop jumping about. She'll look you straight in the eye. "Oleg? Oleg only wanted what was best for me, you know. He had a job to do. He was under orders—and I know this because he whispered it into my ear more than once—to find three stray dogs and train them for the mission. Only one would be chosen. The best. The most courageous. The most stoical. His superiors were very intelligent people who did wonders for Russia. They were highly skilled mathematicians and told him that even he could be of use to Russia. I'm telling you, I have fond memories of Oleg Gazenko. Sure, he could be hard on the three of us, but did he have a choice? We had to move forward, always higher, always further. One day, some people in white smocks came into the laboratory. I was in my little box. Albina and Muchka, too. They were misbehaving. The people in lab coats were giving us dirty looks. Oleg was uncomfortable. He spoke to them for a long time. One of the men lost his temper. He pointed at a calendar on the wall and began to shout in his Moscow accent. He stomped his foot on the floor. There was a picture of people riding a tractor on the calendar. It said, "Comrade! Respect the five-year plan!" Then Oleg became very nervous. I could sense—because I can sense things like that—that he needed me right at that very moment. Up until then, I had depended on him for everything. I was at his mercy. I sensed that I at last had the chance to give him back a little of all that he had given me. Oleg and his superiors walked over to our boxes. Albina and Muchka continued to wriggle around. I stayed calm, just like Oleg had taught me. He pointed at me and everyone smiled. Oleg lifted me out of the box. He introduced me to the people in the lab coats, saying, "It will be her. It will be our little Kudryavka!" I had been chosen for something. I didn't know what. Then one of the men said that my name was too complicated, that foreigners wouldn't be able to remember it because they sometimes found Russian names too long and easy to forget. I think that I barked when I heard Oleg say my name. "Laika," someone suggested. "Everyone will remember that. It's easy to pronounce." They all nodded in agreement.

And that's how I became Laika.

The Laika stamp. Anne Boleyn collected postage stamps, too. She had collected them for years. On winter nights, she would sit down at the dining table and open her album. The project to educate us continued. Homework. My sister racked her brains trying to solve the math questions Sister Monique had set. The queen had understood that she had only a few years to transform us into model citizens. Neatly turned-out, upstanding people. Cartesian beings who knew how to factor an equation. Followers of cold, implacable logic far removed from the folly of Micheline Raymond, professional cook. It wouldn't be wrong to say that Anne Boleyn was my Abbé Faria, the prisoner in the Château d'If who taught Edmond Dantès everything that would make a presentable man of him in the salons of Paris. When his humour permitted, when the shouting died down in the home of the king, we spent our time learning. With the exception of catechism, school projects and home education blended into a single program. The queen would also sometimes immure herself in glacial silence, looking ahead to the end of this exhausting reign and her departure for the southern seas.

I was fascinated by Anne Boleyn's stamp collection. Each little perforated frame brought a tiny slice of the world home to me. One day, we were standing beside her. She had just opened an envelope of Polish stamps. One of the stamps had a stark-naked woman on it, unthinkable for the Canadian postal service. My sister and I giggled nervously, which was enough to out-

156

rage the queen. We must have been eight and nine, and the thought of receiving a letter with a pornographic stamp on it amused us no end. The queen sighed and summoned her reproachful tone. "My God, you are immature. I hope your brother's generation will be more intelligent. It's only a body. There's nothing more natural." Laughing at this body, on the other hand, wasn't natural at all. I imagined my grandmother licking the back of the rude stamp to stick it on an envelope she was mailing to me. "Happy tenth birthday!" Luckily, my grandma didn't live in Warsaw.

Anne Boleyn might have been right. My half-brother was born after the Quiet Revolution. He belonged to an enlightened, free generation. My sister and I still belonged to the old world, polluted by the gospels and the retrograde ideas of a country that was behind the times. Back then, talk of the body, particularly the body in its most intimate moments, was all the rage. The queen followed the trend very closely. The king also seemed to think that describing—sometimes over dinner—the most personal of acts was all part of a child's education. We knew a lot about their lovemaking and their bodies in general. But very little about our own bodies or what we were going to do with them. It was, I think, a generational thing. Upon release from their convents and churches, Quebec's men and women began to go on and on about nipples and menstruation. For a long time, we were told, such talk had been severely punished, and now it was time to talk about such things as often as possible in order to "take back" their bodies and all their functions. Any man or woman who persisted in shrouding their flesh in mystery was considered backward or out of tune with the times. Living under such censure must have been dreadful. The whole thing made me feel so sick that even today I never say "make love." It conjures up, with far too much detail, images of the king and queen's sticky snouts. One day over supper, the king and queen had a bit of a shouting match. If memory serves, they couldn't agree over the man's role in a woman's pleasure. The queen lost her temper. "Women don't need men: we have hands!" I hadn't really understood back then what hands had to do with anything.

Still, I didn't lose any of my enthusiasm for stamp collecting. Noting my interest, Anne Boleyn found me a smaller album and taught me the basics. Mint stamps had to be handled with a little pair of tongs. During these moments of relative calm at home, I felt as though I were travelling alone with the queen. We were the only ones with any interest in the activity. She explained each stamp. Countries used these small paper squares to show off what they considered to best represent their culture. I learned that small, cylindrical red hats were very important to Indonesians. The English and the Swedes had sovereigns of every colour. A green queen. A purple king. In the middle of the table, there was a small pile of stamps from all over, sent to us by an American distributor. Canadian stamps were easier to get our hands on. The queen worked in an office that received letters by the ton. She came home every week with piles of torn, empty envelopes. She soaked the paper in water to remove the stamps, then dried them and flattened them under a heavy book. Sometimes the postmark had spared a stamp or two. They were reused to mail the kingdom's letters. The stamps she recovered had lost their glue, so she had come up with an ingenious solution. She would put a drop of corn syrup on the end of her finger, dab it against the back of the stamp and the corner of the envelope, and stick on the stamp. Canada Post never suspected a thing. The whole time the queen was around, the king never had to buy a single stamp.

On stamp-collecting nights, Anne Boleyn took up the west side of the table, and I, the east. She went about her work meticulously, and I, haphazardly. She had an abundance of stamps, and I, a dearth of them. Her album said *Ambassador* on it. Mine said *Traveller*. Regularity and inconsistency around the same cherrywood table. A rolling stone gathers no moss. The stamps flew between these two political opposites. Our task involved determining which country the stamps came from, asking our adversary a general question about that particular country, answering any questions asked, and attaching the stamp to the corresponding black and white image inside the album, using a little hinge. The prevailing winds came from the west in this country, and so I received many more stamps than she got from me. The white pages of our albums organized the world in alphabetical order—and in English, French-language albums not having arrived yet. In the spring of 1980, country names had not suddenly been magically translated, and the referendum, which had been set to make an ambassador of me, had instead only confirmed my status as a traveller wandering a strange land.

My hands were guided by translations provided from the west.

"Morocco?"

"*Maroc.*"

"*Merci.* Norway?"

"*Norvège.*"

"Ah!"

We devoted entire evenings to sorting foreign stamps that had ended their final journey with us. The queen ordered them from American catalogues.

"Who's the woman on so many French stamps?"

"The Sower."

"Why so many Madonnas on Spanish stamps?"

"The Spanish are very devout."

"Why do the Czechs seem so happy to be driving a tractor?"

"They're Communists."

That was the way of the world. Communists drove tractors.

It seemed to me that the countries included in my stamp album were destined to exist for all eternity. If someone had told me that half of them would no longer be in existence by the time I decided to write about all of this, I wouldn't have believed it. The countries we named in our monosyllabic conversations would all disappear one day.

"Zaire."

"Rhodesia," she replied, not missing a beat.

Puzzled, I went on.

"Burma."

"Upper Volta," she countered, unperturbed.

I wasn't going to let her win without a fight.

"Yugoslavia."

"Czechoslovakia," she said, launching a surprise attack in a calm but measured tone.

I almost lost my footing. I nervously flicked through the pages of my album. Salvation came from the Americas.

"British Honduras," I said, stressing each syllable for effect, sure that this would prove to be the winning reply in our war of words. How could I have been so naïve?

"The People's Democratic Republic of Yemen," she countered, fixing her gaze on me.

Sweating now, I aimed for below the belt.

"The German Democratic Republic."

That was when the unthinkable happened. Beaming like a woman holding a straight flush when everyone else has already put their cards on the table, she floored me with the sublime "Union of Soviet Socialist Republics."

Every syllable still shakes me to the core, even today. Leafing feverishly through my *Traveller* album, unable to find the name of the country that was going to help me find my way out of this predicament, I pretended to have found the fatal weapon and blurted out: "Quebec!"

A tomb-like silence enveloped the whole house in an instant. Eyes dropped to the floor. It was as though a boxer had pulled out a revolver in the middle of a fight and fired a bullet right between his opponent's eyes. I could have lost and kept my head held high. Instead, I had opted for disgrace and a victory without glory. The malicious pleasure of twisting the knife in a wound. The *Ambassador* closed with a thudding sound normally reserved for books of magic spells. The queen stood up and haughtily left the room. She often did that when she heard a hammer word. She would starve us of her presence, holing herself up in a cage of silence and smoking in sadness. I was left alone, just me and my mistake. The long melancholy sigh that had begun on May 20, 1980, and that was to become my family's national anthem, again struck up its sad lament. No one had ever seen the word "Quebec" on a postage stamp. The very idea of it would always be unreal. Almost grotesque.

Looking back today, it strikes me as thoughtless to have included a country that hadn't even dared be born on a list of countries about to disappear from the atlas. Because, of half the countries in our albums, only a handful would survive another twenty years. We didn't know it yet, but it's perfectly possible for countries or individuals to change name and continue to cling to their identity. Because what's in a name, right? How important is it really to insist on being referred to as the

British Honduras, Canada, or Micheline Raymond, professional cook? Aren't these names simply the product of an arbitrary series of decisions, nothing more than a matter of public record? If I tell you, for example, in my most threatening, angry voice, that Sweden isn't Sweden, it's Pumpkin, are you really going to contradict me? No. You'll stick to your position and simply pretend that I'm right. It's just like religion. Because a name, when you think about it, is nothing but a way of announcing to the world what is one day inevitably going to end up on a gravestone somewhere. That was one thing we had to understand in the court of King Henry VIII.

With the queen's sudden departure, a little blue stamp had slipped from the *Ambassador*. It twirled its way across the dining room and landed right beneath my nose. There was the cosmos, set against a background as blue as the Quebec flag. To the left was a spaceship: *Sputnik 2*. To the right, a little pointy-eared dog was staring off at something outside the frame. It was a pretty image. With my translator unavailable, I was forced to conclude that the stamp came from a country called "Posta Romina," that it was worth 1.20 Lei, and that it commemorated an event known as *Primul calator in cosmos*. A blue dog in space? I found no trace of Posta Romina in my *Traveller*, no more than I found Quebec. The stamp's origins were to remain a mystery. The diplomatic incident was quickly forgotten, and that night I fell asleep dreaming that I was in a space capsule high above the Gaspé Peninsula, with a little dog at the controls.

Will you be bold enough to venture back to the wharf in Matane for a fourth time? Perhaps you'll have better things to do. The Gaspé Peninsula is big; there's so much to see. You'll have spent all day thinking of Laika, even while you stood in front of the aquarium at the salmon fishway on the Matane River, where visitors wait patiently for the plucky fish to pass by on their way to spawn. At the sight of so many fish packed into the tiny aquarium, your thoughts will turn to Laika in her centrifuge. Come evening, rather than continue on your way, you'll decide to stop by the bookstore and pick up a dog-training manual, because you've never owned a dog before. You'll head back to the port, once the fog has come in. You'll wait for Laika there. You'll find her in a state of panic. She'll be turning in circles on the quay, barking all the while. "What's wrong, little Laika? You're all worked up!" She'll tug at the bottom of your pants to get you to follow her to the end of the dark wharf. She'll motion out to sea with her head, barking more and more excitedly. You'll see a huge blue and white ship emerge from the fog. Laika will be beside herself. "They're here! They've come back! I'm going home!" As the boat draws nearer, you'll realize that Laika is perhaps no longer in full possession of her faculties. The boat she has mistaken for a Russian ship is simply the ferry that runs back and forth between Matane and Baie-Comeau twice a day. It's late. Usually it comes in at eight o'clock. This evening, it's pulled up to the wharf in Matane two hours late, well after sunset. "Poor Laika. That's no

Russian ship. It's the *Camille-Marcoux*. Can you see the name? It's a very French name, not at all Russian." Laika will realize her mistake. She'll lower her eyes. Together, you'll watch in silence as the cars drive out of the belly of the *Camille-Marcoux*. Calm will return to the wharf. You'll risk a question. "Tell me, Laika. Do you want to see Oleg again? Do you miss him?" Laika will give a long sigh. "Oleg? Of course, I want to see Oleg again. But more than anything I want to see Moscow in the snow. Because, you know, Russia is just as cold as it is here. It was cold in early November when they named me Laika. When the people in lab coats left, Oleg told me that I was going on a long journey, to a place where no living creature had ever gone. I was separated from Albina and Muchka, the pair of them still squealing like rats. There was a trip by truck, then up in a big elevator. Oleg had put me in a cage. Right at the top of the elevator, there was a little round capsule, barely bigger than I was. Oleg glued some electrodes to my chest and suited me up. There were two other men there. As they slid me tail-first into the padded capsule, I understood why only bitches had been chosen for the project. There was no way you could lift so much as a foot. No room at all! Not even to turn round. Oleg patted my head and spoke softly to me. He seemed very sad. He told me I would have a wonderful trip, that I would see all of Russia and all of the Earth far off in the distance. Then he shed a tear. I think he had grown fond of me. At any rate, you had to admit Oleg had done a good job of raising me. When they closed the capsule door, I realized that something wasn't right. I had a bad feeling about the whole thing. I waited for something to happen, for the capsule to start spinning like the centrifuge, for someone to make a sound. Nothing. For two days and two nights, nothing happened. Someone would occasionally pass by the porthole and peer in at me. I barked to let them know I was getting bored, that their game was no fun. Then, on the morning of the third day, there was a noise. Looking out through the porthole, I saw the big elevator get further and further away. Then the capsule started to shake hard, harder than in the testing. I bounced off the padded sides like a ball, I was pressed tight against the floor, unable to move, my heart was racing, there was whistling, explosions, terrible noises. I was sure I was going to die. I could no longer see a thing through the porthole. Everything was going horribly fast. I passed out."

I must have fallen asleep.

When I woke up from my dreams of cosmonaut dogs, I was already running late for school. The yellow school bus was almost there. I missed it. The king had just come back from his night shift. There was no way I could stay home and he wasn't going to drive me. I tried to reason with him. He shouted and roared, started throwing things around. A fork knocked over a jar. He was out of control. His khaki police tie flew in every direction, lending the scene a touch of comedy. A crazy cop. Insults rained down, but I was well used to that. If I wasn't happy, he added, I could always go back and live with my idiot of a mother. A retard like her would have no problem letting me miss school. I seem to remember he gave me a bit of the old "Clear off! Get out of my sight! Shut your mouth! Scram! Now! Damned nuns! Damn it all to hell!" There might have been a few Virgin Marys in there somewhere, too, along with various objects to do with the Church. While it may not have been reasonable, at least his cursing was to the point. I didn't question his instructions, but at this rate I would barely get to school before it was time to take the yellow bus back the other way. Outside, it must have been ten or fifteen degrees below. I set off. It was strange, I thought, that the king had brought up my mother's name. Very strange. The first sign of détente? We'd see. In the meantime, I had ten kilometres to walk, up hill and down dale through the Quebec winter. The Walkman had yet to be invented. Music would surely have made the trek more bearable. I made do with birdsong. After the second kilometre, a miracle happened. The baker pulled up in his truck and asked me what I was doing out on the road in the freezing cold on a school day. I explained the situation. A little taken aback, he cut short his deliveries and dropped me off at school. I was a heavy sleeper at that age. It took a lot to wake me. Not like today, when I wake up shouting several times a night. Although the little blue pills from the Toronto psychiatrist do help calm me.

My sleeping in that morning was never mentioned again. I think the queen must have made a vaguely disapproving remark to the king. As for me, for as long as I lived in the court of King Henry VIII, I never slept in again. I redoubled my efforts in math and strived to work harder at my household chores on Saturdays. The floors gleamed that winter. One day, I wanted to surprise the queen. I waxed the floors that usually she was content to have me scrub while she came along behind me, pointing out the tiny specks of dust she said I'd missed. "There you go again, doing things by halves." The floors shone. You could have seen your reflection in them enough to comb your hair. My efforts did not go unnoticed by the queen. I told her I'd had to get down on all fours. I got what I was hoping for: a smile. It's good to know how to shine a floor, it's a useful life skill, and it makes people happy, too.

Springtime came. Two years had passed since the referendum. I was still collecting stamps. And keeping an eye on the dog in space. It turned out to be a Romanian stamp. As Romanian as Nadia Comaneci. One day when I was alone with the king, I asked him to enlighten me about the dog. Although he could be horrible at times, when he was nice he was very, very nice, and he took great delight in explaining what the dog was doing beside a space capsule on a stamp. Henry VIII never missed an opportunity to teach us something new. I made the most of a Saturday spent baking to ask him my question. Nothing made Henry VIII happier and more considerate than baking bread according to his mother's traditional recipe. He would begin preparing the yeast at eight o'clock in the morning and proudly take the loaves out of the oven six hours later. In fact, there *was* one thing that made him as happy as baking bread: beer. And since he was a practical man, he would often combine the two. The queen would keep well away from him on those days. For reasons I still don't understand to this day, he would often insist that my sister and I stay by his side while he baked. As if to make us believe that our being there was somehow useful, he would ask us to add a little flour or a splash of water. We would feel somewhat useful. He would talk a lot. While the bread rose, he would wait in his rocking chair, reading a biography of the prophet Jacques Brel while he drank. I remain convinced to this day that it is impossible to understand Jacques Brel without a drink in hand.

A twelve-pack would be waiting patiently in the corner. At half past nine, he would crack open the first beer, once the dough had been kneaded the first time. He would be in a mischievous, light-hearted mood. Cue Brel's "Bourgeois" who, like pigs, get stupider the older they get. Happily, cue "Vesoul," too, and we would dance to its dizzying accordion accompaniment in the dining room. Like Brel, we wouldn't be going to Paris, because we couldn't stand the *flonflons*, the *valse-musette*, and the accordion. Fifteen minutes later, the second beer would pick up where the first left off. Cue nostalgia. The king's tongue would loosen; he'd be funnier, too. To the strains of *Rosa, rosa, rosam, rosae, rosae, rosa*, he would recount the hardships of college, the unseen translations to and from Latin that my sister and I would never know since the Quiet Revolution had decided learning math was more useful than dead languages. He would tell us about the priests and the nuns, each less trustworthy than the next. He had flunked his Latin translation at classical college and, the way he told it, this had spared him from the priesthood, a destiny preordained by his role as the family's eldest son. The king never missed an opportunity to knock a priest.

A third bottle would be opened. Cue a little over-excitement. Time for "Marieke," too. He didn't under-stand the parts in Dutch, but that wouldn't stop him belting it out along with Brel like an ode to lost love. It's but a small step from overexcitement to despondency, and the fourth beer helped him get there. "Les timides," those poor tormented men lacking Henry VIII's bravery and brass neck, those poor men who would spend their whole lives shuffling forward, a suitcase in each hand. Cue the flawless portrayal of a bashful man of our own right there in the kitchen, his arms hanging by his sides. Before the fifth beer, the laughs were guaranteed. Then came the tragedy, distinct from despondency with new inflections in Brel's voice. A little anger in *La Fanette*, when he sings that "they had swum so well, they had swum so far that we never saw them again" and of all the times we fail to learn "to be wary of all things." And so the fifth beer would bring us on to "Au suivant," the song the king lived by. He would look us square in the eye, feeling every word, and telling us again and again, articulating every syllable, that it's more humiliating to be followed than to follow. I would wonder when the king had ever followed anyone. Sure, he had had followers (all of the female persuasion), with dozens more to come, but I couldn't remember him ever following anyone.

"Les toros" would follow. The same anger, but this time washed down with a sixth beer. A second round of kneading, a second batch of bread rising. A baking interlude that restored a little of the king's sobriety. By then, the afternoon was upon us. Between the sixth and seventh beer, the king would slump into an inebriated gloominess that made him resemble Jacques Brel more closely than ever. The same hangdog eyes. "Les filles et les chiens" didn't help. At this point, his resentment would be focused on things my sister and I didn't have the faintest idea about. Fortunately for us, the eighth beer would be knocked back to "Plat pays," a land that would temporarily lose its Belgian identity and become the enigmatic place where the king wound up whenever he drank. Because it was there, just at the bottom of the eighth beer, that we would start to lose him. He would begin to lift up off the ground, rising ever higher, ever further, until we needed a telescope to watch him ascend into the sky. The rest would come to us in snatches. The ninth beer. "Quand on n'a que l'amour." The poetic trance and the insults began. "You don't understand a thing!", "You're always talking behind my back," the outlandish "Keep slapping on the makeup like that and you'll end up pole dancing!", and the hilarious "Get your nose out of that book or you'll turn into a priest!" The king would be raving by now. He still managed to guzzle a tenth beer to the sound of "Une île," that tropical destination just off the coast of hope, where he swore he would finish his days, not in this land of weaklings too scared to stand up and be counted! The bread turned golden in the oven while the sailors of Amsterdam blew their noses into the stars. The king would be in orbit. Then, the final nail in the coffin. The bread cooling on the counter. The king staggering between the fridge and the sound system. Speaking a language that he alone understood. Our kindest words would sting him hard. Then, the twelfth and final beer, leading straight—do not pass Go—into "La Quête," played loudly enough for the devil himself to hear. Pity the wretch who failed to recognize this song as the most beautiful thing ever written! Pity the wretch who failed to touch the unreachable star! Might the ground open beneath his feet! Might white mice infest his home! The king would lie down on the sofa and fall into a deep sleep. There was no waking him. Only the queen would manage to get him up one hour later. He would retire to his bed, completely spent.

Baking bread is exhausting.

Alcohol dug an unfathomable chasm between him and the rest of the world. And it was alcohol that put the first cracks in the wall of power that he formed with the queen. Little by little, beer fractured their agreement, breaching the wall for me and my sister to slide out.

When sober, the king would be one with Anne Boleyn, forming a cold, authoritarian whole. But add a little wine or beer and the king would leave the queen's gravitational field to become another, a star free to roam the cosmos. The most scathing of the attacks launched after the ninth beer included "I never even wanted kids" or the inevitable "Once I have my boat, no one's ever going to talk to me like that again." This little game played out more often over winter than summer. The last half-hour the king spent awake would be absolute torture for the whole court. The more he drank, the further he drifted away from us, moving elsewhere, north or south, it didn't matter, to someplace where we were not. And when it was wine he drank, the trip would be all the quicker. As the years went by, he became ever more hurtful before passing out, ever more cutting, harder on everyone. The king drank only on Saint-Jean-Baptiste Day, Labour Day, Christmas, New Year's Eve, for the entirety of the local shrimp festival, on Workers' Day, Thanksgiving, the Immaculate Conception, the feast of St. Blaise, at baptisms, weddings, funerals, while nodding off, filing his tax return, watching television on a Sunday evening, talking on the telephone with his brothers, learning to navigate a boat, at sunset, when visitors came, when visitors left, on election night in front of the television, on winter days when he stayed home because he wasn't working, during construction work, at family suppers, at police get-togethers, and during the summer holidays.

Otherwise, Henry VIII never touched a drop.

The king would stay sober over Easter at his mother's, the only person in the world who could still claim to have the slightest influence on his alcohol consumption. When he was with her, he only drank half as much. The queen, meanwhile, veered back and forth between being sad and taking her anger out on us. How many police officers have turned into alcoholics from listening to Jacques Brel, I wonder?

And so if we wanted to make the most of his mental state to get detailed answers to certain questions, the window of opportunity was between the second and fourth beers. "What's the USSR?" There were pictures of the May 1 parade on television. I saw an orderly country. The Red Army marching in perfect formation. Everyone seemed so happy.

Even the intercontinental ballistic missiles seemed happy.

My father didn't need to be asked twice. "It's a country that has rid itself of its torturers, one where all are equal, where everyone has access to first-rate health care, and where the education system is vastly superior to our own. In the USSR, there's no such thing as private property. People are appreciated on their merits and all look to the future together." It was blatant provocation. "Could we move to the USSR?" How come he hadn't thought of it earlier? "No, that's not possible." He told me that the Soviets—supermen if you asked me—had sent more than a few vessels into space, vessels that were sometimes manned and that had names that set me dreaming. *Sputnik*. "They even sent a dog into space. Into orbit. Laika was her name. I think it was *Sputnik 2* or *3*."

It was the dog on the Romanian stamp.

I began to envy the little dog that the finest Soviet minds had dragged away from a life of mediocrity down here on Earth. There was no way that she would ever feel the little earthquakes up there in *Sputnik 2* or *3*. Cut off from the entire planet, she was turning silently, in the delicious solitude of a satellite, now immortalized on postage stamps. I kept on dreaming of Laika.

You'll dream of her for a long time, too. Long after she'll have explained to you that she came to once she was in orbit around the Earth. "You don't know what weightlessness is," she'll coo in her Russian accent. "You just float. Life loses all the heaviness that makes people sad and tired. I could see millions of stars on the other side of the porthole. It's simple: take the number of stars you can see from your home on a summer evening and multiply it by one thousand. That's what it's like. Oleg had been telling the truth: I could see all of Russia from up there. But not only Russia! The whole world was right there. I saw North America pass by four times. Then, it began to get hot. Very, very hot. The tube they had given me to eat and drink through began to heat up, too. I could barely breathe. I stopped barking. The air in the capsule was so warm that I could no longer keep my eyes open. I think I must have fallen asleep. When I woke up, I was on the deck of the *Pavel Ponomarev*. The sailors weren't paying me the slightest bit of attention. I think they must have fished my capsule out of the sea. I looked for Oleg everywhere on the ship. He wasn't there. Nothing but brutish sailors getting drunk on vodka all day long. When they had drunk their fill, they began singing such sad Russian songs. The drunker they got, the sadder the songs. Does that make sense to you? Drinking to make yourself sad. As though there weren't already enough reasons to be sad in Russia! The ship docked here one morning. I thought I was in Murmansk. As soon as they let down the gangway, I ran out onto the wharf. I looked everywhere in this town for any trace of Oleg. He wasn't to be found. I must have left the ship at the wrong port, I thought to myself. But by the time I got back to the wharf, the ship had gone. I barked for hours because I could still see it off in the distance. I'm sure they'll come back. Oleg must be looking everywhere for me. He must be so proud of me."

You won't dare contradict her. You'll think back to the Romanian stamp, which you might also have had when you were young. Plucking up your courage, you'll try to convince Laika it would be better for her to come back into town with you because it's cold at the port. That the ship might not ever return. You'll reassure her, telling her there's no vodka or sad Russian songs where you're taking her. She'll shake her head. "Impossible! Listen, you're very nice and thank you for the meatballs, but I can't leave. I know they're coming back. Just think about it! They didn't save me from the freezing streets of Moscow only to forget me here. I'm sure I cost them far too much for that. It just doesn't make sense... When you make such an effort to train a dog, to teach her how to sit, to sit up and beg, to keep calm in a centrifuge, you can't just leave her in the port in some unknown country! I'm much too important to them! They'd never do that to me. I guarantee it: A Russian ship will be here to save me by tomorrow. I'll miss it if I leave with you now. I'll miss my chance to go back to Russia! No, truly, you're very kind, but I think I'm going to stay here." Then you'll be sad. Sad she won't follow you. So much so that you'll wonder which of you needs the other most. Did Abbé Faria need Dantès as much as Dantès needed Abbé Faria? Was Oleg really so attached to Laika? Does a queen become attached to her subjects? You'll leave the port of Matane—and Laika—behind.

*In the thick cold of oceans' languors.*

It wasn't until later that the meaning behind my first dreams of space was revealed to me in an assignment set by our geography teacher, Mr. Ferguson. The instructions were vague: "Write a research paper on a foreign country." It was a wafer-thin excuse to get us into the library and have us copy out paragraph after paragraph from an encyclopedia. It kept us occupied, and gave the lackadaisical teacher plenty of time to go for a smoke outside. The girls immediately opted for countries with names shrouded in an aura of grandeur or exoticism. "I'm gonna choose Austria, just like in the movie *Sissi, the Young Empress.*" "I want to do the United States—

that's where the bionic woman lives!" "It's Australia for me. I've always wanted a koala." Every choice set off a chorus of "Ahhhs!" or "Shoot! That's the one I wanted!" The boys' choices reflected their wilder nature. "I'm choosing Germany. Because of the bombing." "I want Japan because my dad just bought a Toyota." A few poetic souls went for names that sounded nice—or that sounded funny, like Togo or Cuba. Each was given his or her piece of the planet according to criteria every bit as valid as those at the Yalta Conference. "And what about you?" the teacher asked me, itching to go outside and eager to ensure no one would sit idle during his brief absence. Only one choice seemed possible. I had to get to the bottom of things. Since I had illusions of grandeur and was always keen to impress, I replied, "The Union of Soviet Socialist Republics," which was greeted with general hilarity since my classmates had never heard of the country and thought I was joking at first. The professor was already hunting for his lighter in his pockets and replied, "Very well. If you want to make life difficult for yourself." He headed out of the library, leaving us to fight over the encyclopedia volumes. My claim to volume U went uncontested. Our little Austrian, a girl from a well-off family who had fallen for the charms of Sissi or the Von Trapp family, was horrified to find she had to share a volume—and a desk—with the bombardment-obsessed Germany enthusiast (*Autriche* and *Allemagne* both beginning with the same letter in French). She spent the remainder of the school year trying to convince us she'd had no choice. The centre pages—which they had to hold up in turn in order to read and write down the information on their respective countries—kept falling, and this awkwardness was reflected in their work. The histories of both countries were reduced to hopeless gibberish, so much so that the teacher unearthed gems like "Bordered by Italy and Denmark, Germany is known for its great composers, Bismarck and Adolf Hitler."

My assignment was a resounding success. I got the highest mark in the class. On the cover page, I used up almost one entire red crayon colouring in a map of the USSR. If I squinted hard enough, the country looked like an elephant, its trunk the Kamchatka Peninsula. I had also confirmed the origin of my little stamp. It was indeed the little dog, Laika, that the Soviets, to the world's great surprise, had sent into space aboard *Sputnik 2*. My stamp came from Romania, friend to dogs and the USSR.

What was most important to Laika, aside from the extra treats it earned her, was the petting and the con-gratulations that came every time she did what she was told. Dogs aren't aware of the future the way we are. They have short memories. If you go out to the bakery for twenty minutes, your dog will greet you when you come back as though you had been gone for three days. When dogs are taken from their mothers, they have no memory of her at all. (Apart from cosmonaut dogs—they remember everything). They have no idea what will happen in two days' time. They recognize a handful of people they see often. But that's the extent of their social life. What they love more than anything is seeing their owners happy. If you happen to be sitting on a sofa, all alone in your apartment, and you begin to cry as you think back to the past, your dog will take pity on you and put his little paw on your toe as though to say: "I don't know why you're so sad. We've just eaten. The sun is shining. The leaves on the maple trees outside are rustling in the July breeze. We're together. Let's go for a walk!" The dog makes no distinction between the simple past and the present perfect tenses. It doesn't grasp that the simple past is used to speak about something that happened only once and that the present perfect describes a past action that may well be repeated in the future. I like to imagine that, just as they closed the space capsule on Laika for the last time, she began to suspect something was up. When the force of the acceleration on liftoff pinned her to the padded floor of *Sputnik 2*, Laika must have given a little yelp. Then she heard a long whistling sound.

A few hours after *Sputnik 2*'s launch, the Soviets announced what they had known from the very beginning. Laika wouldn't be coming back to Earth. *Sputnik 2* wasn't designed for a return flight. All the scientists knew this, even Oleg Gazenko. The dog was to die, poisoned after ten days. Years later, scientists no longer moving within Russia's orbit revealed some horrifying details: Laika had probably survived no more than a few hours aboard *Sputnik 2*: a malfunction had caused the temperature inside the capsule to soar to 41 degrees Celsius and she had literally been baked alive in the sun's rays. She died of fright and heat. I am quite certain that Laika, sweating, thirsty, and overcome with the heat, three seconds before her last breath above our atmosphere, thought back to a dark Moscow street half buried under the snow, a stone's throw from Lenin's tomb. She must have felt something approaching nostalgia for the cold. A lingering scrap of humanity. Just like when the Little Match Girl gave up the ghost in the Scandinavian cold, perhaps she saw her mother's face in the Russian sky, right above the colourful onion domes of St. Basil's Cathedral. But there'll never be irrefutable proof of that. I suppose.

When he wasn't baking or holding forth on the virtues of planned economies, the king would take us down to the port in Matane to see the cargo ships. More often than not, they were ships under the Liberian flag come to take stacks of logs back to England. On this particular grey Sunday, we also expected to see an old African boat, rusted and haunted by smiling sailors. You could see nothing but their eyes and teeth in the darkness, the king said. Well used to the routine, I stared out over the raging October sea, hoping a sea monster would loom up out of the water and gobble me up, swallowing whole the fate I no longer had any desire to meet and freeing me in the process. Our car drove onto the wharf just as I was reaching the conclusion that this whole place and this family must look much nicer from space. A mental orbit.

When I opened my eyes, the Soviet flag was fluttering in front of the red Volvo. *I will come like a thief in the night.* The Kremlin had answered my prayers. Help was at hand. Elbows resting against the ship's rail, three wise men smiled down at us. My heart was pounding. Another more naïve boy lacking in foresight might have run out to the end of the wharf shouting, "Take me with you! Take me back to Leningrad!" We stayed there for a quarter of an hour in the drizzle, looking through the blue curls of my father's cigarette smoke at the three men waving down at us.

That night, Baikonur was the setting for a dream that I still have often to this day. My psychiatrist is very fond of the dream; it's one of his favourites. I'm lying down in my space suit. My cosmonaut helmet has the letters CCCP on it.

"Control tower to comrade Dupontov. Are you ready for liftoff?"

"*Da!*"

The countdown begins.

"ПЯТЬ, ЧЕТЫРЕ, ТРИ, ДВА, СТАРТ!"

They say the cosmonauts were thrown back against their seats by a force equivalent to an elephant sitting on their chest as their rockets accelerated. They could only sit, immobile, while they waited for the unbearable pressure to end. They also say that the acceleration stopped suddenly, at which time the cosmonauts' bodies would empty through every gushing orifice. There are no pictures, of course. It's surprising to learn that the body's first reaction in the absence of gravity—far from its planet of origin, in other words—is to vomit violently. That empty feeling.

An alarm clock thrust me into a yellow school bus and my classmates' sarcasm. Julie Santerre had a field day. "You look depressed. Did you lose another referendum?" In my waking dreams, I programmed the trajectory of a Scud missile from a nuclear submarine straight to her house. A smoking radioactive crater would be all that remained of her, her Canadian flag, and her collection of Nathalie Simard records.

That same evening, my father told me he had gone back to the port to see the Russians. "They're all crazy about maple syrup. They drink it by the glass!" By the glass? Did the world really need to know that communism had managed to put a dog into space to understand that there was currently a shipload of supermen in our port at the end of the world?

My plan was simple, and I wasn't going to waste any time putting it into action. My bedroom down in the basement was separated from the rest of the family by the ground floor, a buffer that would guarantee my successful escape. All I had to do was not fall asleep. Once everyone was in bed, I pushed back the covers, still fully dressed. I had a bag full of the bare essentials at the ready: a can of maple syrup (to bribe the sailors who would find me hiding in the hold), my assignment on the USSR (to prove my unequivocal commitment to my new fatherland), a pair of mittens knitted by my grandmother (you never know), and the stamp with Laika on it (my passport to this socialist paradise).

In silence, I closed the basement door for the final time, took out my union-made bike as quietly as I could (pushing it along on its rear wheel so that the tic-tic-tic didn't alert the neighbour's dog), and went for one last ride along the roads of this damned country. In the dark night, under a million stars, I rhymed off the names of all the Soviet republics out loud to give me courage. From west to east: Lithuania, Latvia, Estonia... On my way down the hill—the hill that would lead me to freedom—I felt the salty air of the St. Lawrence press itself against my face and I thought to myself that the feeling of acceleration couldn't have been very different to that of my own *Sputnik* lifting off. Giddy with speed, I cut through the air on my bicycle. The fog patches made it feel like I was passing through a bed of clouds. Suddenly a flaw in my escape plan threatened to spoil everything. How was I going to get on to the ship? It was much too tall, and the port of Matane wasn't exactly coming down with ladders. Hergé had the answer. In *Prisoners of the Sun*, Tintin, my childhood hero, clambers aboard a ship by grabbing on to a mooring line. This rope would be my Ariadne's thread to the heavens. The rest would be down to diplomacy. All I would have to do is crouch down under the tarp of a lifeboat and bide my time until the cargo ship reached open water. Once it would be too late to turn back, I would emerge from my hiding place and demand to be brought to the captain. I would explain myself to him and, upon my arrival in Murmansk, I would be taken straight to Moscow, possibly aboard an Aeroflot plane, where Leonid Brezhnev himself would welcome me in person. He would understand. My eight-page assignment on the USSR would allay any doubts. I'd become the first Quebecer to join the party ranks and, after an intensive Russian course (courtesy of the superior education system), I'd take a *Sputnik* flying class. They'd pull out all the stops to launch the first cosmonaut from Quebec (or Canada, depending on what the Yvettes made of it). The possibility of meeting the same fate as Laika didn't dampen my enthusiasm. I'd die in space, in a blaze of glory. To my tearful family, having followed my *Sputnik*'s launch from their living room, the Kremlin would send a letter containing, essentially, the following:

*Moscow, June 16, 1982*

*His Royal Highness King Henry VIII,*

*Your son has made the ultimate sacrifice for the USSR. In his honour, Red Square will be renamed Dupontov Square. His death, just like Laika's, is proof that communism is a seed that grows in the hearts of all those who thirst for justice. Should you look to the sky on a star-filled night, perhaps you will see zipping eastward over the Matane*

185

*sky what you will take to be a shooting star. In fact, it*
*will be a Sputnik piloted by your son. Rest assured that*
*Sputniks now come equipped with an undercarriage. Your*
*son will no doubt be tired after the journey, but you can*
*console yourselves with the thought that at least you don't*
*feel any earth tremors when you're weightless.*

*Leonid Brezhnev*
*Communist Party Secretary*

*P.S. Thanks for the maple syrup.*

The envelope would have a stamp of me on it, wearing my CCCP helmet with the Earth in the background. That's all it would take for the king to raise an army of the proletariat to march on Ottawa and demand the government immediately recognize the People's Republic of Québec, no strings attached. Triumph. Singing in the streets. Tears of joy.

The fog lifted over Matane, and I entered the deserted port. A salty halo left an aura around each light. Out of breath, I walked the last hundred metres. I couldn't allow myself to be intercepted so close to my goal. The smell of fuel oil drifted along the wharf. Right where my ship should have been, I saw nothing but an all-too-inviting void. I was rooted to the spot. Shivering in the mist. A stranger came up to me on the wharf. He was wearing small round glasses and holding an empty cage. "Time to go home, little one. Your ship has sailed. Maybe another time. You didn't happen to see a little dog? A little mutt?" He'd been coming down to the wharf for days now, he said. He'd met a little Russian dog there. A funny character. He looked a little like me. Like a tireder version of me. Thinner, too. Like a distorted reflection in a dirty mirror. There's no more terrifying sight for man than catching a glimpse of his future self.

I ran to my bike and cycled home broken-hearted. I'm telling you, that man didn't seem at all normal. In the morning, I got out of bed on time. I haven't missed a bus, a train, or a plane since. I'm a model of punctuality, wherever I go. Because, as we all know, punctuality is the politeness of princes. When you're the king's son, you make sure you're on time.

So you're still here, are you? Still looking for her? What do you expect her to say? "Hey, it's you again! Well, you're patient, aren't you? Have you come to wait for the ship with me? No, it still hasn't arrived, but it won't be long, trust me. Oleg will be back. He'll take me with him and we'll go home to Russia. I won't be staying here long; I can promise you that. This isn't my country. I'm not at home here. I don't understand the people here." If you ever pass by the port of Matane again, it would be very nice of you to make sure she has everything she needs. She's still waiting. That's all she knows how to do, wait for the boat that will take her far from here. The big journey to the unreachable star. She's very well trained, you'll see. She can do all kinds of things.

CHAPTER 5

# The Hens (1982)

FOR MY TWELFTH BIRTHDAY, Henry VIII gave me twelve hens. It was, he said, time for me to take on my *responsibilities*, and the birds were the perfect way to teach me. Some fathers try to do the same by offering their children a magnificent pony or a gleaming moped to ride, making all the other children instantly envious and proving key to their popularity in the schoolyard. The idea of becoming a teenager while raising poultry left me skeptical, but I was willing to give the king the benefit of the doubt.

When Jewish boys turn thirteen, they celebrate their bar mitzvah, where they are given the world on a silver platter. The world or a condo in Florida, depending on the family's means.

In our house, it was hens that were given. By the dozen.

He had chosen Rhode Island Reds, perfect for budding poultry farmers looking for high egg returns. Hens of this breed lay somewhere between two hundred fifty and three hundred eggs per year. A phenomenal return. Rhode Island Reds are considered docile and low-maintenance. Now, I'm willing to take the farming brochures at their word, but after my terrible experience with hens in 1982, I swore never to encourage the reproduction of what I still to this day consider to be feathered vermin. The Rhode Island Red is the state bird of Rhode Island. Naturally. It had no say in the matter.

In practice, I think the hens were a roundabout way for the king to put me back in my place.

The village school had no shortage of children who worked on the farm, morning and evening. With calves, cows, pigs, and broods to take care of, *they* hadn't had to wait until they turned twelve to familiarize themselves with farming life in Quebec. In some cases, they carried the odours of the farm around with them on their clothes. A waft of manure hung in the air of our yellow school bus every day. It emanated from the Desrosiers kids, the unpleasant gang of boys who called the shots at school. I seem to recall at least one of them committing suicide before they turned twenty-one.

The stout and sturdy Nathalie, who had made fun of me from day one, showed no signs of letting up. Like a hunted animal, I desperately sought a way to shut her up once and for all. As it happened, the poor girl had a pungent stable odour about her. One day, as I was walking behind her, I held my nose, hoping the other kids would ridicule her. But a little brat squealed on me, and it was she who left me covered in bruises. Nevertheless, my efforts were not in vain. Some of the other mischief-makers, who hadn't dared stoop so low to ridicule someone, made the most of the breach I had made in our school's decorum. It didn't make much difference that Nathalie had now joined the ranks of the students who bullied me.

I told the king the whole story. He was livid. There promptly ensued a sermon on our farming roots and my nasty behaviour. The king reminded me in no uncertain terms that a single generation separated me from the farming world and that by insulting Nathalie I was insulting my grandfather, too. "Fair enough," I didn't dare reply, "but she stinks." I didn't see how he could compare my grandad Léo to that foul-smelling witch.

I realized I had genuinely wounded the king's pride and that he wasn't going to let it go. Even so, it took two years between Nathalie's assault on my olfactory senses and the arrival of my hens.

For some, existence consists of either being put in their place or putting someone else in their place. The game is over when everyone has been put back in their place, when everyone understands their role in the great pecking order. I think that's more or less what the king was trying to make me understand.

Reading about the USSR had introduced me to *kolkhozes*. I consoled myself with the thought that my henhouse brought me closer to a true socialist existence. The goal of my poultry farming was to turn a profit I didn't have the slightest intention of sharing with anyone. And I didn't have five years to carry out my production plan, just one summer, which—as defined locally—lasted from July to August. I was going to have my work cut out. I would have to come up with egg-shifting strategies to make my business profitable. The formula was simple: The basic equation Revenue – Expenses = Profit (Loss) $(R - E = P)$ would have to lead to a positive result, otherwise I'd be in the red and the experience would turn out a failure. I was put in charge of accounting, marketing, customer service, production, henhouse management and upkeep, egg-gathering, egg-storing, procurement, human resources, and advertising. The P variable was going to depend on neighbourhood egg sales.

One April day, I heard that my red super-layers had arrived. Not knowing what to expect in the shed that had been renamed "the henhouse," I lost myself in conjecture. I had carefully prepared their new abode, even helping the king build a yard with wire mesh next to the henhouse where the birds would be free to roam to their heart's content, safe and sound out in the open air. They could go back into the henhouse via a small hole in case it rained or they were attacked by a coyote. Secretly, I considered myself lucky he hadn't decided I should take up dairy farming.

The hens were delivered in cages. As soon as they were set free in their Poultry Palace of Versailles, I felt myself invested with an authority I had never known before. I was responsible for these living creatures. This feeling of omnipotence is one any child at that age can aspire to. I could have been looking after a dozen zebus, a dozen amoeba, or a dozen Danish princesses and it wouldn't have changed a thing. I reigned over a dozen living organisms and, aside from the obvious mercantile considerations that were going to control the entire operation, the experiment also had the unspoken aim of putting me face to face with the divine order of Creation. The king had briefed me on the rudiments of poultry farming. It wasn't rocket science. The birds needed very little looking after. Before going to school in the morning, I would have to feed them and change their water. Then collect the brown eggs they had laid in the nest box. Once a week, I was to give them a mixture of powdered sea shells to help them produce solid shells of their own. Poultry farming seemed to require nothing more than consistency and daily attention. The twelve red sisters explored their new surroundings, clucking with pleasure. It didn't take long for one of them to discover the feeder and begin to peck away at it, quickly followed by the others. Hens are like that: they learn by imitating each other. But unlike stray Muscovite dogs, there's only so much they can be taught. I was learning myself as I watched them. At first, back in the early days, I couldn't tell them apart.

But then I began to recognize their individual features. I even gave them names. And here I must admit that I was petty enough to name them after my classmates. After I had fed them in the morning, I would stay on to watch them. I soon noticed that they kept pecking each other. At first blush, it seemed as though each hen would peck the neighbour that happened to be closest. I was wrong. After a few days, I realized that one of the hens would peck all the others without ever being pecked back. On the other hand, the smallest of the lot would constantly be pecked by all her sisters without ever daring to peck back. I christened the group leader Madame Nordet. Then came Julie Santerre, the teacher's pet, who—behind a veil of patience—would take the constant pecking from her superior only to wreak her revenge on the other ten. Next was Brigitte, Julie's friend. Then Isabelle, pecked at by Madame Nordet, Julie, and Brigitte, and pecking away in turn at all the other hens. And so the pecking order continued, right down to the group's long-suffering much-pecked member, who remained nameless, such was the extent to which her fate depressed me.

There is little to warm the heart in the apotheosis of animal stench.

In the little fenced-in yard, shouts echoed off the school wall. The schoolyard was a sad place where tensions between the village and rural parents were atoned for on a smaller—albeit no less cruel—scale. I learned all kinds of fascinating things there. Some children's parents, for instance, were convinced that police offi-cers pocketed the fines they handed out for themselves and that this was how they were paid. And so the day the king came home with a second-hand Volvo, they shouted at me that the car had been basically stolen from the people of Saint-Ulric. Or rather they didn't shout. They grunted, and the grunting was followed by a shove to the ground. As a narrative epilogue to the violent episode, they shouted "faggot," a word whose true meaning I was unsure of and that never failed to spark a deep epistemological crisis. For the longest time, I thought that a faggot was someone who knew how to read. I tried to explain that, in point of fact, police officers' salaries were paid by... But really, what was the point? I remember complaining to the king. He con-sidered what I'd said without responding.

In the early hours of the morning, I continued my observations in the henhouse. The twelfth hen didn't seem to be suffering unduly from the treatment dished out by its fellow creatures. Around mid-May, all the hens began to lay eggs. Enormous mutant eggs too big for the egg cartons and with up to four yolks each. I set the price at one dollar twenty-five for a dozen. I col-lected seven dozen eggs a week, which in theory should have earned me eight dollars seventy-five. But the hens easily ate ten dollars of feed per week. I began giving them table scraps to satisfy their hunger. You'll be sur-prised to learn that hens aren't picky eaters. They eat ham, beef, and even any chicken you throw at them. The queen was extraordinarily helpful. She managed to sell at least three dozen eggs a week to her colleagues. She convinced them by pointing out the savings they would make. My Rhode Island Reds were laying like crazy. It was a summer of omelettes, pancakes, and soufflés.

This new source of protein coincided with the proclamation of a new royal edict. The court had decided that I was to take up weight lifting. "Girls like big guys," the king had insisted, in response to my dubious look. "And you'll knock the teeth out of the guys giving you a hard time!" The king showed me photos from a body building book. To prove it was more than just empty words, he came home one night with a collection of bars, weights, dumbbells, and a weights bench. The basement had become a torture chamber. The decree was remarkable in its precision and in how doggedly the king applied it. There were to be three weight sessions every week, at exactly the same time on Mondays, Wednesdays, and Fridays. For reasons beyond me, my sister was exempt from the edict. And so thrice weekly, Henry VIII would choose a series of exercises for me in *Body Building for All* to put a bit of flesh on my bones. The names of the muscles provided me with a new form of poetry. Words like trapezius, rhomboids, short abductors, deltoids, biceps, pectorals, and quadriceps brought new-found complexity to my anatomy. Until then, I had never claimed to be anything other than a slightly more masculine version of my mother. Rediscovering her likeness in the mirror every morning provided me with no small consolation, but now the king's exercises were encouraging me to cast a more attentive eye over my anatomical destiny.

Impossible to ignore, the bench, bars, and dumbbells waited outside my room, neatly lined up on a carpet the colour of goose shit. They were my passport to peace in the school henhouse. I forced myself to do the exercises, more bored than I'd ever been, casting longing looks at the books I no longer had time to read and that the king wanted to keep me away from. While my Rhode Island Reds laid their eggs, the king and I pumped iron.

Unfortunately, the natural balance of my flock was rudely disrupted. One day, the king, the queen, and the little brother came back from Matane carrying a suspicious-looking cardboard box from which emanated some high-pitched cheeping sounds. The little brother, who was now four, had been unable to resist the charms of a squawking brood of twelve yellow chicks a farmer had been doing her best to get rid of. My hens had naturally been receiving a lot of attention over the previous two weeks and some of this celebrity had begun to rub off on me. The little brother hadn't taken kindly to being outshone by a dozen miserable hens. So he had kicked up a fuss, citing favouritism and demanding they buy him a dozen little chicks so that he, too, might reconnect with his farming roots. My little brother's whim had, however, been founded solely on aesthetics. He lost all interest in them as soon as the chicks lost the fine yellow down he had fallen so hard for. As chance would have it, the chicks belonged to the same breed as my American super-layers. We kept the little ones in the basement under the heat of a lamp beside my room—right beside the dumbbells—to make sure they had everything they needed. At night, I could hear the cheeping of little orphans desperate for a mother figure. I aimed to reunite them with their kind as soon as they were big enough to live alongside the adult hens. The charming chicks, now featherless, had morphed into hideous bald little creatures, somewhat grotesque and very awkward, teetering on disproportionately long legs.

The time came to merge the two flocks. I dreaded that morning every bit as much as my first holy communion. The chicks were now almost fully grown, a little scrawnier than their counterparts outside in the henhouse, but their family ties were plain for all to see. One morning, after gathering thirteen eggs that probably contained eighteen yolks in all, I decided it was time for the big reunion. As usual, when I went into the henhouse, the bigger hens crammed themselves into a corner, a few of them pecking at the feed. The scrawny younger ones ran around in a cardboard box, obeying their own anarchic choreography, their gaze filled with a mix of apprehension and hope for the future. In a few short seconds, the air would be filled with the sound of joyous clucking, chickenspeak for words of welcome. I set the box down. What happened in the minutes that followed still haunts me at night. The new generation rushed off into a corner, the young hens piling atop each other in a noisy panic while their blood sisters ignored them. The little ones were scared of the bigger hens. "For the love of God, what's wrong? Aren't you all the same breed? You can teach them to lay eggs! Show them the rules of the game in this world of yours!" My twelve feathered apostles turned a deaf ear. "It's only a matter of time," I thought to myself. "Soon, they'll form lasting friendships and there'll be a coming together of generations as never before. In three days, they'll all be wondering how they ever coped without each other."

I boarded the school bus in the morning to the amused looks of the other children. Curiously enough, becoming the leading egg producer on Route 4 had done nothing to boost my popularity. When I walked by with the perplexed expression of an anxious zoo keeper, I'm sure I heard them cackle like hens just to tease me. The Desrosiers brothers were the worst. For years, they'd endured the taunts of the other kids because they didn't have a telephone at home. In 1982. By choice. Anyone looking to communicate with them had to go over there and knock on their door. As was often the case for the police, according to a reliable source.

My new farming pursuits left me tired for school, where unusual things began to happen. Outside in the yard, groups formed according to the strangest criteria. Most of the time, the strongest boys and girls, no matter which grade they were in, would surround a kid and give them a hard time. The victim was not chosen at random.

First off, they had to make sure the parents of the child they were going to bully didn't work for the school or the school board. Little Jean Beaulieu was thus spared, since his mom, who held a teaching certificate, regularly came in to substitute for teachers who called in sick. The girls who hung out with Julie Santerre were also spared; that went without saying. And, of course, these pogroms also spared anyone who had an older brother or sister capable of inflicting painful reprisals on the bullies. I often managed to hide in a corner or demeaned myself sufficiently to claim I belonged to Julie Santerre's group. As soon as I lowered my guard, a circle would form around me. At that particular instant, not unlike crows or starlings, threatening heads would spout forth cries of persecution that reminded me of the sounds the damned hear on their way through the gates of hell. Whenever I tried to break my way out of this hellish enclosure, I would be shoved back into the middle and the insults would fly. They tended to be unsubtle comments about my lisp, report card, or—there was that word again— faggots. I should never have let on that I enjoyed reading so much. On these occasions, I would sometimes think back to the Sermon on the Mount and Sister Jeannette. Her memory brought comfort to me, though it never managed to break the senseless chain that had me sur- rounded. Happily, every other day another boy would take over at the bottom of the pecking order. His name was Étienne. He was an only child, and rumour had it that he played with lacy dolls at home. I found this regrettable, but not to the point of burying his face in the mud, which happened to him regularly. It was thanks to him, I think, that I worked out that "faggot" didn't mean "a keen reader" because Étienne was such a bad reader he failed grade six. But that hadn't kept him out of the sights of the Desrosiers brothers and the other boys. Whatever they meant by the word "faggot," I didn't want to be one. Not even for the Kingdom of Heaven.

One night when I was struggling to lift the hundred-pound bar with all my might, the king provided a few clarifications about faggots. A man in Saint-Ulric had left his wife and children, he said, because he was now a "faggot" and had gone off to live with another "faggot." I imagined they both worked in a library or collected dolls. One day—I don't recall why—the man in question came to our house. I think he'd been talking to the police; someone had stolen something from him. He had come to give the king a document. I was out on the main porch, in front of the dahlias. He was in a car with another equally well-coiffed man. They were smiling and seemed very happy. He waved at me before they drove off. Two men in a car, smiling together on a sunny country road. For a long time, I thought that's what being a faggot meant. It didn't seem all that bad.

The king explained to me that faggots were mentally ill and didn't want anything to do with women. Jacques Brel was therefore not a faggot, even though women seemed to turn him down a lot. Since it involved abandoning wife and children, I wondered if the king might be a faggot. But that didn't make any sense. Far from turning women down, he seemed to want to say yes to all of them. None of this was of any use to me in the schoolyard. One day, I made an amateurish mistake. I was hiding behind a wall. My usual tormenters appeared from nowhere. It was a classic clobbering, now that I think about it. In full accordance with best practices. A number of neutral observers witnessed the scene and decided to have a word with Madame Nordet after recess. She looked exasperated. She quietened everyone down and said, "You're all going to have to acknowledge your wrongs and forgive each other for being so horrible. That's what Jesus would have done. Eric, we'll start with you." And I had to tell my tormenters I was sorry. I asked them to forgive me for being at the foot of a wall that clearly belonged to them.

One morning in June, I found Julie Santerre surrounded by her friends. They had laid enormous eggs and were waiting there in silence without pecking each other. It was very strange. Something was up. The smell of calamity hung in the air, along with the usual henhouse stench. One of the young chicks lay dead in the corner, covered in blood and pecked all over. The eleven young chicks who remained were huddled on top of each other, trembling in one corner of the henhouse. The beaks of the adult hens were still stained with blood. There had been carnage. The clucks from the murderers chilled the blood in my veins. I gave the poor martyred chick a Christian burial. The king, always a valuable source of advice on such matters, decided that a protective fence was to be added to the henhouse, at least until the chicks were big enough to defend themselves. This was done. In their avian ghetto, what they gained in safety they lost in freedom.

Segregation is not limited to humankind.

Julie Santerre went on clucking and laying eggs, sometimes rubbing up against my leg as I emptied the nest box. It felt good to kick her away. She would go off to peck Brigitte or Nathalie or one of the other hens. It was at that moment, in June, that I lost all affection for my hens. I think they could feel it because the shells on the eggs they laid grew harder and harder. School was over. I thanked God. It was Saint-Jean-Baptiste, Quebec's national holiday, a day that also marked the start of the shrimp festival. Along with demolition derbies, the festival was the society event of the year in Matane.

It's thanks to the Northern shrimp that the rest of the province of Quebec has heard of Matane at all. A local revealing his place of birth to the suburbanites of Montreal will often be met with a stream of idiocy. "Aha! Shrimp. Ha! Ha! Ha! Hello there, Shrimp! Ha! Ha!" (To any readers tempted to read this exchange out loud, the laugh must be *completely* inane.) To which the man from Matane would love to reply, "Shut your face!" but instead comes up with an off-the-cuff response that is witty and courteous in equal measure, "That explains my rosy complexion, I guess..." He knows it's futile to point out that the shrimp in question come not from Matane but from Quebec's Lower North Shore, and that their only tie to Matane is a seafood-processing plant down by the port. The shrimp festival was thus not a celebration of the birthplace of shrimp, but rather of the place where they held their breath, were steamed alive, and were then shelled between a factory worker's fingers. So, in June, as soon as school let out, Matane would dance with shrimp. Literally. A mascot named Claw roamed the town's streets, pinching passersby. Do shrimp even have claws? A fact little known to festival-goers is that the Northern shrimp (*Pandalus borealis*) is protandrous. This means that it's a hermaphrodite and that its male organs develop and become functional before its female organs. It reproduces and then goes through a short transition period before spending the rest of its life as a female. We usually eat shrimp when they're female. With cocktail sauce.

The festival organizers came up with a little song that I must confess I still know by heart. We were taught it at school. A little ditty about how welcoming Mataners are, one big happy family that likes to drink and dance and eat shrimp. Don't laugh, it doesn't sound any better in French.

Now, everyone knows you can't have a festival without a parade. St. John the Baptist had fallen out of favour, thanked for his loyal service to the people of French Canada. Which meant that the annual parade in his honour had been cancelled. His absence left a gaping hole in the list of rituals that punctuated life in our town by the water. To fill this yawning void, the town authorities had organized the festival parade. Truth be told, they made only slight changes to the old Saint-Jean-Baptiste parade. Neither the route nor the crowds that turned out to see it changed. Now, at this point in my story, it's vital that a brief explanation of the organizing committee behind the Matane shrimp festival be given. The shrimp festival had been co-founded by Benoît Bouffard in the 1960s. Benoît Bouffard was a descendant of the six Bouffard brothers who married six sisters from the Durette family a century earlier. One set of siblings coming together with another. Hence, no doubt, the festival slogan—"Say hi to the family!"—and the line in the theme song, "We're all family here." The committee democratically elected the festival chairman, or chairwoman, every year. This individual's name and photograph were then published in *La Voix gaspésienne*, making them famous overnight. It was, after the town council, one of the most prominent offices in town and a gateway to celebrity. The post was so important that the chair almost never went uncontested. Elections were held in due form, with all kinds of conspiracies and machinations employed to secure the ultimate post. Sometimes I wondered if, as an adult, I would be made of the right stuff to one day chair the Matane shrimp festival. I had my doubts. But since I left Matane long ago, the question is now moot. The festival committee invited the whole "family" to come watch the parade from either side of Rue Saint-Jérôme. In the event of bad weather, the event would be held the following evening instead. Normally empty sidewalks bustled with people from all over, from neighbouring parishes, Rimouski, the Matapedia Valley, and even visitors from Quebec City and Montreal as they began their tour of the Gaspé Peninsula. By seven o'clock in the evening, a crowd was already waiting patiently outside the Dalfen and Continental, two department store chains where you could buy made-in-China nail varnish, toothbrushes, and polyester underwear, all at bargain basement prices. Faces turned pink in the wind waiting for the ceremonies to begin. The municipal police had closed the street for the occasion. We were there because it was the place to be. Right there by the bridge over the Matane River, where a handful of salmon fishermen were still sloshing around in the rapids. The clamour of the crowd suddenly reached us. We applauded the first group of majorettes wearing microscopic skirts, twirling their wooden batons in the northerly skies. Divisions of army, sea, and reserve cadets then followed, all in neatly pressed uniforms. There were also frightening clowns who tried to draw laughs from the crowd with their improvised tomfoolery. Among them, the famous Tit-Pit Leduc, lantern in hand, put in his annual appearance. Tit-Pit Leduc was always dressed up as a bum and I often confused him with Sol the clown, whose record I had at home. Julie Santerre's figure-skating team performed—to the great delight of all the older gentlemen—a few charming pirouettes. The crowd was jubilant. Carnival floats! Yes! In downtown Matane! Floats! The Optimist Club. The Knights of Columbus. The Daughters of Isabella. The Women Farmers. All of them waving to the crowd. It was possible to deduce, with a bit of simple arithmetic, that everyone who lived in Matane was either in the parade or on one of the sidewalks on either side of the road. In the distance, we could make out the little tower on the armoury, the words *POST OFFICE* engraved on it for all eternity, despite the fact that no one in Matane spoke English. The Bouffard dealership paraded huge American cars that people caught on camera, Instamatics at the ready. Flash bulbs. The excitement built. From the top of the street, applause and cheers went up, announcing the highlight of the evening. Yes! There it was! The shrimp was back for another year. It was at least ten metres long and two metres high. Lying on its back and smiling to the crowd, its casual pose signifying that good times had come to Matane. On either side of its body, four long pink legs fluttered in the breeze. Its broad smile and fleshy lips offered the promise of salty kisses. Its big wide eyes were as blue as the sea. The crowd roared with delight as it passed by. Ecstatic children followed in its wake. "Thou shalt have no other gods before me." But we didn't care about the Ten Commandments. It was time to party! Dance, Gaspé, dance! Dance until your arthritis or your cirrhosis forces you to sit back down again! Dance before your youth ups and leaves on you! Dance before winter comes back! Slowly, the monstrous crustacean brought the parade to an end. Shrimp were then served to the festivalgoers in glasses and eaten from the end of a toothpick. A voice wished everyone a wonderful festival and they all headed home.

Aside from that, the shrimp festival didn't mean much to my sister and me. Most of the activities were held at night, boozy affairs at the "Lumberjack Camp" or one of the local bars. *Proudly and generously sponsored by Labatt Breweries.* Even though the voice of Jacques Brel was nowhere to be heard, the king was a big fan of the shrimp festival. Empty bottles littered the festival site every morning. People staggered home. Drink to the tune of a rigadoon!

Summer took on the shape of an egg. The hens laid furiously. I kept on pumping iron in the basement. I still hadn't knocked anyone's teeth out. A few eggs ended up transformed into muscle. For two weeks, the poultry farm almost broke even. Sometimes my leg squats hurt the cod scales that continued to grow behind my knees. As I crouched down, I could feel a slight tearing of the skin, right where the scales shone brightly. They were on my elbows, too. In other parts of the world, my scaly secret would have been common knowledge, but it continued to go unnoticed here in the north, where we had to cover ourselves up, even in July. I stayed strong in the face of distraction. Poultry farming. Reading. Body building.

Then came September 1982.

There was a new boy in my class at school. He was older than everyone because he'd flunked a couple of grades. He also wore a black leather jacket. He looked toxic from a distance. His arrival completely upset the pecking order. He was now at the top. His name was Jimmy Côté, and he didn't have much of a sense of humour. Rumour had it he'd done time for petty theft. He came from a family that could boast it always had at least one member behind bars. The king knew them well. It was the king who warned me about the boy one day. I wasn't to go near him. Jimmy Côté would spend only one year at school in Saint-Ulric, even though I seem to remember him being there forever. From the very first class, Mr. Ferguson, a rather strange teacher, spelled it out for him. "You don't call the shots here. Do I make myself clear?" Mr. Ferguson wasn't one to mince his words.

Back then, if there was one thing I feared more than nuclear war, it was finding myself alone with Mr. Ferguson. He taught English, phys ed, and ecology. He would often tell us terrifying stories about his experiences with parapsychology. Because Mr. Ferguson was one of Saint-Ulric's mystical figures, and very much into spiritualism and dowsing. Sometimes he would interrupt English class to tell us he was talking to dead people or capable of astral travel. He could, in other words, leave his body whenever he pleased and float through the air like a ghost to keep an eye on what others were doing from a distance; a little like God, but a member of the teachers' union all the same. I envied Mr. Ferguson's ability to leave behind a place he didn't like, if only in spirit. I kept looking until I found a guide to astral travel in the library. Readers were warned of possible dangers—the practice could sometimes lead to madness—but I was willing to take the risk. It involved, if I remember correctly, relaxing and spreading your fingers apart. This way you obtained a kind of translucent ectoplasm that could float through the air, pass through walls, drift along the St. Lawrence to Rivière-du-Loup or someplace else, all the way to Russia. It could go far, very far.

Despite my efforts to go undetected in the schoolyard, Jimmy Côté was always popping up nearby. First, he wanted to be sure that I was, indeed, the son of Henry VIII. Then, with the help of other birds of a feather, he made it clear that uniforms were a sore point with him. For me, 1982 was the year of stomach-clenching cramps. Not a day went by without an ambush, not a single recess was terror-free. I took refuge in the henhouse.

There, too, things were beginning to fall in around me. The rate of lay had plummeted with the cold nights. One morning, death visited my hens for a second time. It was the little brother who came running back in from the henhouse, panicked by what he had just seen there. The temperature had dropped below zero during the night. Clearly no one had ever explained rigor mortis to him. At a loss for words, he lay down on his back and showed us that one of the hens had taken up the very same position and was refusing to budge. The hen must be dead, we explained to him. "It can't be," he maintained. "Its eyes were open."

I investigated. A hen had indeed died during the night. One of the younger ones. There was no sign of injury. A perfunctory autopsy revealed that she had been bitten from behind. The king suspected a weasel. The other hens went about their business, blissfully unaware. I had a new enemy to deal with.

Things began to heat up at school. Jimmy and his gang of mercenaries had taken over the schoolyard. Mr. Ferguson's ghost stories seemed to have little effect on them. One day in October, the tension reached boiling point. With my thoughts consumed by my hen's murder, I had forgotten my fear of Jimmy and didn't see him and his gang walk over. They began with a few slaps I didn't see coming, a classic technique. I don't know what came over me that day; I think the weasel affair had left a bitter taste in my mouth. Not that I was overly fond of my hens. Truth be told, they were a lot of work and were becoming harder and harder to look after. No, on that particular morning, I was mostly thinking about the nasty weasel and its treacherous attacks, and I felt an anger the size of a pea forming somewhere deep inside me. The pea grew, filled out, and took on a personality of its own that had as many qualities as flaws. Without really understanding why, and without really looking up, I grabbed Jimmy's first apostle by the throat and held him tight until he began to turn blue. The colour went perfectly with his eyes and shoes, I thought. A touch too pale, perhaps. A deathly shade of blue would suit the little blond runt to a T. I would have to tighten my grip a little. Julie Santerre and her chicks would usually cheer on battles and acts of violence against me, cackling: "Blood! We want blood!" This time, they were there all right, but they were so astounded, they'd been struck dumb. It was as though it was *their* necks I was gripping in my hand. They didn't come to the wretch's defence, nor did they encourage him to kill me, as was their wont. Jimmy Côté, completely taken aback, made no move to step in and help out his vassal, which speaks volumes about honour among hoodlums. The boy was slowly turning blue right before my eyes, while I marvelled at just how strong my arms were. I silently thanked Henry VIII for getting me into body building.

This flash of manliness was proof positive that integration is possible, no matter the setting, provided you make a little effort. The pecking order wasn't set in stone, after all. A simple throttling was enough to rejig it. No need for anyone to lose any teeth. Julie Santerre and the chicks still didn't say a word. I could feel the heat rising from the kid's neck beneath my fingers. His carotid artery was throbbing right where my thumb and index finger met. His pulse was racing. I wondered if he, too, was going to fall on his back, eyes open, teeth clenched. He was so thin. Just a few more weeks' training, I thought to myself, and I'd be able to snap his neck with one hand. I imagined the cracking sound his vertebrae would make as they snapped. Whispers went up from the students crowded around me. Someone prayed to God. The aesthete in me still wasn't happy with the colour of the little hoodlum's face; his skin was so soft and pale. I'd never thought of him as good-looking, but now the blond kid almost moved me to pity. My breathing accelerated. A girl cried out.

I felt a powerful hand grab my wrist. It was Mr. Ferguson. A ghost must have tipped him off. The dead always rat on you. Ironically enough, my victim, the fair-haired boy, was the one who found the drowned sailor's body on the beach. Had he shouted so loudly that day because the sailor's blue face prophesied this October morning in 1982 when he was almost choked to death? Can you read the future in a winkle? Mr. Ferguson, who must have eaten his own fair share of eggs, separated me from my victim. Colour was slowly returning to the boy's face. I stood there, breathing hard, arms by my sides, in front of Julie Santerre and her chicks, Jimmy Côté and his hoodlums, and Mr. Ferguson. There was a deathly silence. And yet I wasn't thinking of them at all. I was thinking back to the soft, throbbing neck of that little fair-haired boy; to our breathing, together as one; to his beautiful blue eyes rolling back in his head; to his hair, as fine as the hair on the heads of Étienne's dolls; and to his pink-blue lips, the colour of winkles.

The incident had the effect of a nuclear bomb going off in the schoolyard. The kid got his breath back and walked off, helped by his companions. Julie Santerre and her chicks had, for once, ceased their morning cackling. Surprise and bemusement being the usual way for poultry to grasp reality, the birds remained stunned for a while before they returned to their pecking. The sweet smell of death, like the promise of as-yet-unexplored pleasures, seeped into this scene from life on the Gaspé Peninsula. Mr. Ferguson was furious. I didn't care. I was on an astral journey of my own. Since he was in communication with the spirits, I would have liked Mr. Ferguson to assure me that, one day, the memories of Saint-Ulric would be nothing more than sorrowful archives. Everyone has archives. The problem with my own is that every little tremor sends dust flying from the hundreds of volumes. It gets right up my nose, chokes me, and forces me into a cleaning spree.

Funnily enough, no one ever called me a faggot at school again.

The weasel, on the other hand, continued to prey on my mind. The henhouse massacre continued. Each morning brought with it a new corpse. The weasel attacked only the weakest, which is to say, the younger chickens. I didn't get it. Had it been wolves or other birds, the threat would have been wiped out with a few pecks. The hens were huge and there were twenty of them against a tiny weasel. They had already proved they were vicious enough to kill one of their own to defend their territory. With a little intelligence, they could easily have made a midnight snack of the weasel. But there you have it: hens aren't very bright. Thousands of years in captivity has turned them into morons, to the extent they couldn't care less if they see one of their own die right in front of them, just so long as the pecking order is respected. They'll offer up the weakest—"Kill her! Kill her!"—without realizing they themselves will be the weasel's next victims. I now know that every omelette, every angel cake, every soufflé, and every bucket of Colonel Sanders' fried chicken brings us closer to a better, more intelligent world, where cruelty and pettiness do not exist. Reader! Have some chicken tonight without the slightest remorse! Vegetarians! Join our ranks and unite your digestive tracts against them! As with every great revelation in life, it took an animal as mundane as the hen to get me to see the light. One night, I came home from school to find my hens plucked and frozen. The king had butchered them. He had chopped all their heads off. One after the other. The heads were stacked in a pool of blood. I saw in Julie Santerre's lifeless eyes the imminent end of Anne Boleyn's reign and Jane Seymour's accession to the throne.

We weren't out of the woods yet.

At school, the pecking order had changed. I was no longer part of it. I wasn't at the bottom, and I wasn't at the top. I was in a class all my own. The blows I had once received were now destined for Étienne. I couldn't do anything to help him. Only watch. There's only so far an attempted murder can get you in a henhouse that size.

I never, ever, made fun of the smell of manure again.

# CHAPTER 6

# The Great Horned Owl (1983)

BEFORE THE WHITE MEN ARRIVED, the Gaspé Peninsula was inhabited by the Micmac. Slowly driven southward by European colonization until they were finally confined to reserves, these first inhabitants had already named rivers, bays, and capes. For example, in the Micmac language "Matane" means "beaver pond." The Micmac were particularly close to the wildlife of the Gaspé Peninsula. In addition to their hunting grounds and the land they lived on, they left us legends about moose, owls, and belugas. At school, the Gaspé Peninsula's first inhabitants were never mentioned. Before the English, there had been the French, and before the French, there had been the Indians. There were no Indians anymore. "They left," we were told. I remember occasionally wishing I were an Indian.

Legend has it that the Micmac thought the wind came from a huge bird beating its wings. It seems only natural to me that the Micmac were behind a legend about the origin of the wind: their ancestral lands were, and still are, exposed to very strong winds, which blow relentlessly practically every day of the year. It would have been strange indeed if the folklore of the First Peoples hadn't mentioned it. According to legend, there had once been a huge bird on the Gaspé Peninsula that would frantically beat its enormous wings, giving rise to gusts so strong that they stopped the Micmac from taking to sea to go seal hunting. It was decided that someone would have to find the bird and break one of its wings to put an end to the wind and allow the people to hunt so they could eat and clothe themselves. A hunter set out to find the animal and managed to break one of its wings. Dumbfounded, the bird stopped moving altogether. The wind died down all across the peninsula. Not another breath of air. The Gulf of St. Lawrence, as calm as a mirror, took on the exact colour of the heavens, so much so that there was no longer any way to tell the sky and the sea apart. The currents slowed to a standstill. The gulf became a huge pool of stagnant water, which the marine life deserted in no time. The people living beside the water understood too late that all life comes from the wind. The Micmac hunters, a little sheepish as one tends to be in such circumstances, called on the elders who, in turn, called on Glooskap, creator of the universe, the earth, and humankind. According to the myths behind the creation of the universe, Glooskap had created men and women by shooting arrows at birch and ash trees. The Supreme Being, reluctant to intervene where man had clearly erred, denied the elders their request for help. What men had broken, they would just have to put right themselves. And so other hunters were sent out in search of the wounded bird. When they found it, they captured it and cared for it. Once the bird was better, they set it free again, asking it to kindly beat its wings a little more slowly so they could live and fish in the Gulf of St. Lawrence.

The French, English, and Irish settlers never had time for Micmac wisdom. The Europeans came with their own myths, crucifixes, and gospels. The great bird's existence was quickly forgotten as they set about clearing the land. But they didn't clear everything. In 1983, particularly on the Gaspé Peninsula, there remained huge swaths of woodland that still had the power to amaze the Europeans we sometimes send postcards to. In these infinite expanses of evergreen, knowing how to find your way around is crucial. The First Nations, it seems, relied on the internal compass that lives in each of us. Henry VIII, who wasn't Micmac, had learned how to use a real compass as a boy scout and had decided in 1983 that it was time for my sister and me to learn how to use one, too. And so he decided to organize a trip into the forest. The land that stretched out behind our house would do. First, we had to find a point on the horizon. A peak-shaped clump of trees right at the top of a hill.

Between it and us stood fields, a river, a forest—the usual scenery.

Using a Silva compass is quite straightforward. A metal needle floats in a bubble of water. The red side points to magnetic north, which, where we were, was around fifteen degrees off true north. A dial shows the number of degrees to magnetic north. Since the needle always points north, it is possible to work out the angle between the direction you are walking—assuming you are walking in a straight line—and the line between the compass and magnetic north. The compass also comes with a sight gauge. By placing the compass on a horizontal surface below eye level, you can work out the angle between magnetic north and where you want to go. If you can't see where you want to go, you can also use a topographic map that shows degrees, minutes, and seconds, so that you'd have to be a complete idiot to get lost. The king had perfectly mastered the technique of finding his way around with a compass. It was agreed that we would set out around 1800 hours to reach our destination at approximately 2100 hours. As a precaution, the queen agreed to send us a signal from the dining room at 2100 hours precisely. She would flash the lights on and off three times. This signal would be clearly visible from on top of the mountain in the shadows of the woods.

We were very excited. The king never took us anywhere by himself. Since we had left Rivière-du-Loup, the queen had come along on almost every activity. I was intrigued by this sortie with Henry VIII. Once out of the court, the king became a very different person. He talked differently. He seemed freer, in a way. He would spend long spells in silence during which his thoughts would wander, far, far away. It wasn't the beer. The king never drank when he was on the move. But as soon as he sat still for an hour, he would start looking around for a bottle.

He had us take the azimuth. The azimuth is the angle formed by the destination, you, and the magnetic north pole. Three points are all you need. After that, once you start walking and have lost sight of the destination, you need to take shorter azimuths. For example, let's say, dear reader, that your goal is to reach a point whose azimuth is 160 degrees. You start walking. You know where you're going because when you left you established that the point you want to reach is 160 degrees off magnetic north. But for one reason or another you lose sight of your destination. A forest, a ravine, or a mountain suddenly stands between you and your goal. Don't panic. Get out your compass. Using the sight gauge, turn the dial to 160 degrees and find an immovable object (a tree, a rock, a church) in your line of vision. Now you know that if you walk toward this object, you'll move closer to your destination in a straight line. Proceed until your destination comes into view. You can't go wrong.

First we walked across fields. It was easy walking because nothing was growing there. Sometimes the owner would rent the field out to another farmer to grow barley. In those years, a golden plain would sway gracefully behind our house. The fields, the king taught us, were rented out because the small local farmers couldn't afford to buy all the land they needed for their livestock. Another oddity was that no one built in the field. And yet the ground was nice and flat—it would have been easy. Henry VIII explained to us that in the past, anyone at all could have bought themselves a field and built whatever they pleased. Now it was against the law. All of Quebec had been divided into white and green zones. You were only allowed to build in the white zones. Otherwise, you had to let the land lie fallow or grow something. You were, however, allowed to walk wherever you wished. I found it all very strange. The country was huge, and yet you weren't allowed to build on it as you pleased.

There was a small river at the end of the field. We could hear it babbling before it came into view. It didn't have a name. It cut across fields and hills and probably flowed into Rivière Blanche or the St. Lawrence. A tiny drop in the Gaspé Peninsula's water system. A number of wood cabins stood along the river. More shacks than houses, these uninsulated ramshackle homes were lived in by young families in the summer; families who, when winter came, sought refuge in miniscule apartments in town or in the village of Saint-Ulric. In the fall, the homes were heated with wood stoves. The chimneys gave off white smoke. Through the trees, the tiny homes looked like something right out of a fairy tale. Their inhabitants were on welfare; in other words, they didn't work. The king and queen didn't seem to approve of their chosen way of life. I would often hear them complaining about what they called the "welfare bums." The king would quote Félix Leclerc: "The best way to kill a man is to pay him to do nothing." There was no shortage of welfare bums in Saint-Ulric and Matane. They lived in a kind of parallel world. We were allowed to speak to them, but the king discouraged us from becoming too friendly with their children. Henry VIII ranked teachers, singers, and farmers very high on his world hierarchy. Welfare bums were right at the bottom. I slowly learned how to spot them. It wasn't very difficult, a bit like birdwatching. You just had to drive around with the king and wait for him to point out a welfare bum to know how to recognize one. At the time, in Saint-Ulric, we still had to share our telephone line with two or three families. We couldn't use the phone whenever the line was busy. As I recall, we once had to share our line with a family of welfare bums. I heard the king complaining that no one would ever be able to use the phone in our house because those people had nothing better to do than spend all day on the phone with other welfare bums. The party line also allowed us, provided we went about it very carefully, to listen in on other people's calls.

The river people, as we called them, were jobless. They ate canned food and often didn't even have a phone. Compass in hand, we passed by a cabin where a little boy lived. He would walk across the field every morning to wait for the school bus at the side of the road. He was feeble, pale, and sickly. We often saw him throw up in the snow whatever he had just eaten as he waited for the bus. His parents were very young. The mother was often ill, stretched out on a makeshift bed in the darkness, occasionally finding the strength to moan. Behind their cabin there was a henhouse, where turkeys, ducks, guinea fowl, and hens lived together in perfect anarchy. A flag with the fleur-de-lys on it hung as a curtain in the window. By the river, three or four rickety cabins—some with floors, others without—were home to other families who drew their water from the river. A parallel society lived there, far away from modern city life. At another time, in other circumstances, social services would have had the entire neighbourhood evicted, brandishing some act or other to protect something or other. It was a little corner of the third world, right here in Canada.

At school, the little boy was often spotted in the company of other children "of that breed," as the king and queen referred to them. Two girls from Saint-Ulric, a redhead and a brunette, had taken him under their wing and saw to it that the others didn't peck at him too much. Sometimes I would listen in on the conversations in their corner of the henhouse. They would often talk about their parents' right to raise their hand to them. According to the two girls, it was perfectly normal. Almost all of the other children in the group agreed with them. Someone suggested that it was perhaps wrong for a father, even though he was head of the household, to beat his children, or anyone else for that matter. The two girls responded angrily. A father, they said, had every right to bring his children to heel. For instance, one of them told us her dad had thrown her down the stairs the week before because she had answered him back. Her companion added that her mom and dad beat her regularly. They were both proud to come from families where their parents still did things the good old-fashioned way. Their testimony reduced the other children to silence. So as not to question their convictions, we agreed with them: "Of course, if they want to, they have every right to. No one should ever take that away from them." At times like this I thought that, all things considered, life in the court of Henry VIII wasn't so bad after all. In the yellow school bus on my way home, I imagined Henry VIII with a whip and stool, trying to bring someone to heel. It made me laugh. I often think back to those two girls who, now in their thirties, must be running after a child somewhere, broom in hand, as they fondly remember their father standing at the top of a staircase, his eyes bulging with rage. I'm glad I don't have any children because there's a huge wrought-iron staircase where I live in Montreal. It turns twice on its way down to the sidewalk. It has thirty steps. It was around 1975 that Child Protection Services was created in my province. And apparently since its creation, children have tended to walk rather than tumble down the staircases of Quebec.

The king didn't call in on the river people. Their little community didn't interest him. So we crossed the bridge to the forest. There, we lost our azimuth a few times. Through the fir, white cedar, and spruce trees, we stumbled around blindly in the soft light. The odd startled partridge would take off at our feet. Such noisy appearances by the birdlife froze the blood in my veins. I felt as though I was no longer at home, that I had desecrated somewhere sacred. Henry VIII told us that scarcely twenty years earlier he had been forbidden from hunting these partridges, but that Americans had been able to buy the right to hunt on stretches of land as big as Belgium and keep out Canadians who wanted to hunt. Salmon, moose, deer, and partridges had belonged to the Americans. But things had changed, and now we had the right to hunt and fish on our own land. Which was only common sense, I thought.

At last, we stepped out into a clearing. It was, in fact, a long corridor that had been cleared and that divided the forest in two. In the midst of this long strip, which stretched for thousands of kilometres, loomed tall steel towers connected by power lines. Henry VIII had us admire them and listen to the hum of the transformers. It was a worrying kind of everlasting music. He looked us right in the eye and told us that these towers carried the electricity produced by our nationalized hydroelectric power plants. Nationalizing them had cost a fortune, he stressed. Today, people in Montreal and far-flung Gaspé paid the same price for their electricity, and no one had to go without. Sounding sympathetic, he told us that villages in the sticks had once depended on sleazy dam owners for their electricity. These swindlers, who had also come from the United States, English Canada, and even England, had gotten rich on the backs of the people.

Evening came. We clambered our way up through the dense forest. The king no longer spoke. A bird hooted, softly and deeply. It sounded almost human. Then we saw it. The great horned owl.

The great horned owl is native to the area stretching from the northern tree line to the plateaus of Brazil. It is at home all across North America. You'd be surprised how tall it is. Sixty centimetres of plumage from head to tail. Its wingspan reaches one hundred fifty centimetres in flight. Great horned owls do not build nests. They commandeer the nests of others, where they lay and sit on their eggs. Unlike the brown-headed cowbird, they sit on their own eggs. They let others build a nest before throwing them out on their ear.

No matter where your travels might take you in North America, you can hear their clear hoot from dusk till dawn. You'll know it when you hear it. It's a clear and pure, almost artificial, hoo-hoo-hoo-hooo sound. The bird's size and its song announcing the onset of twilight are amazing. But it's neither size nor song that impresses ornithologists: it's the bird's migratory habits. Because great horned owls do not migrate. They are born, they live, and they die in the same place. Unlike other birds that change latitudes to satisfy their hunger, great horned owls never feel the need to move. They never get itchy feet. Their food supply allows them to live sedentary lives. They live on rodents, other birds, hares, small farmyard animals, and even cats and dogs. Working their way to the top of the food pyramid has enabled great horned owls to adapt to their habitats. Their position in the food chain has left them indifferent to the life cycles of insects and the growth periods of plants. A genuine threat to any small animal, great horned owls have learned that if they are to stay put, they must eat their neighbours. And they give no quarter. Few other birds have their capacity to adapt. Man is their main predator. They also have a surprising ability to adapt to all types of climate. From the chilly forests of the Rockies to the bayous of Louisiana, great horned owls feel right at home. From time immemorial, the hoots of great horned owls have swept across the vast land where I was born, across entire time zones, from the beaches of Newfoundland to Vancouver Island. Their song, along with that of the white-throated sparrow, makes up the soundtrack to our countryside. Whenever you hear their morose lament, you'll know that you're in my homeland.

When it spies its prey on the ground—still blissfully unaware of its fate—the great horned owl opens its wings and glides down in the darkness. A second before it seizes the rodent, it lets out a piercing shriek to stun its victim. The animal is paralyzed, unable to flee as the great horned owl grips it vice-like in its talons. It might be a field mouse, but the great horned owl tends to prefer larger prey, like hens or hares. It doesn't matter how big they are: great horned owls can carry away prey two or three times their weight. In the warm, living flesh of its victims, the great horned owl has found an alternative to the nomadic ways of most birds. It stays at home and devours its neighbours. This stroke of genius is worthy of admiration in itself. So when we saw it perched on a birch tree in the twilight, it seemed to be saying, "I'm staying put. I've been here since before paper was invented. You can nationalize the land all you like; it is of no concern to me. I was here before you were, and I'll eat the last of you before taking back these forests." Years before a teacher handed me Baudelaire's *Les fleurs du mal,* I understood the meaning of his "Owls," these strange gods that sit in meditation, darting their red eyes. His verses, in a nutshell, encourage us to stay right where we are. "Man, enraptured by a passing shadow, / Forever bears the punishment / Of having tried to change his place."

Henry VIII had clearly never read Baudelaire. Or hadn't spent enough time on his owls. He must have preferred "A Passing Glance" or "A Carcass." We were living the final days of Anne Boleyn's reign, apprehending it though not yet fully aware of it. Soon, the wind of Jane Seymour would rise up and sweep away all before it. A time of horrible infections and decomposed amours was at our door.

The hoots of the great horned owl accompanied us to our destination. We were on top of the mountain, our azimuth. The sun was sinking ever deeper into the St. Lawrence. On the other shore, the first lights were beginning to sparkle in Baie-Comeau. Down below, Route 4 and its houses, no two alike. I could see our white house quite clearly, my white henhouse with its idiotic Rhode Island Reds, and the big white shed where Henry VIII was building his boat, his great dream. Then the "green" zones, the welfare bums by the river, the forest with our very own partridge, and the nationalized Hydro-Québec towers. Everything the king had showed us that night, the whole country. I thought to myself that it was all very well, but we hadn't really learned anything. I thought that the king might have made a bit of an effort and, rather than taking out his compass to show us a lot of things we had seen thousands of times before, he might have, for instance, simply lit a fire at home and explained to us, before the flames, why he had always voted for René Lévesque. I didn't see what the walk was meant to teach us about our province's modern-day history.

Anne Boleyn, the queen of punctuality, turned the lights on and off in the dining room at the agreed hour. Three short flashes, three longer ones, then three short ones. An S.O.S. in the Quebec countryside. Night fell. We gazed at the world spread out before us as though for the last time. We had to start heading back through the forest. We were in for a few surprises on the way home. I realized that the forest, once plunged into darkness, becomes another place governed by other masters. As the sun's slanting rays fall, the great horned owl regains control over the darkened land. It's also at this clammy hour that certain mysteries of our existence are revealed to the mortals that dare venture deep into the shadows.

There comes a time in every boy's life when he realizes he always has been and always will be trapped in a forest forever. Whether he is born in the foggy port of Amsterdam, in the paddy fields of Indochina, or on the still-forested edge of the New World, there's no escaping this fate. There will always come a time when, amid Glooskap's vast creation, the boy will contemplate the profound solitude of existence. For some, this moment, which is as important as all of the Holy Church's sacraments, comes on a football field or in the thin arms of a tall blonde whose heart isn't really in it. In my case, it came that night in the forests of the Gaspé Peninsula. We descended into the shadows of the night, lighting the way with police flashlights. Taking an azimuth was out of the question. Compasses have the drawback of being useless at nighttime, when your destination lurks in the shadows. In such circumstances, all you can do is trust your senses and the lay of the land. Since we had followed the road the whole way up, it seemed obvious to me that the best way home would be to take the same route. But local forests are dense. It's easy to lose your way, and our king has long legs. He doesn't always wait for his subjects in the mad dash onward. My foot slipped on a moss-covered rock, and I fell face first into the frightening autumnal darkness. In the pitch dark, the noises of the forest took shape, amplified by the ancestral fear that has accompanied them since the dawn of humanity. Man may well be able to send faster and faster rockets into space, build bigger and brighter cities, and put up longer and longer bridges, but a mere hoot from an owl in the depths of the Canadian forest will always make his blood run cold.

When I came to, the king and my sister had disappeared. I was alone between two fir trees. I had lost the compass and the flashlight. The nervous flapping of a bat out hunting between the treetops set the tone. The great horned owl sent out its sad lament. I had never heard it so close. What you first notice about the great horned owl in the dark of night is its two piercing eyes that sweep down upon you like misery onto humanity. Before you realize what's happening, it's already too late. The bird was perched on the branch of a nearby fir tree when I opened my mouth to cry for help. Before I could even let out a cry, it opened its beak to speak. Now, there will be those among you, dear readers, a marginal minority—albeit a noisy, troublesome one— who will refuse to hear what the great horned owl has to say. Such people are easily identifiable by their grey clothing and the terse creases that form around the corners of their mouths when they reach their twenties, while their peers are still smooth-skinned and youthful. They're the type who never eat dessert. Easily recognized and therefore avoided, this species is not completely without merit, since it excels in other spheres of human activity, such as designing forms for the revenue ministry and drawing up management policies for computerized data collection protocols and running supply chains for petroleum derivatives. These people will dismiss the great horned owl's speech out of hand. But at this point in my story, there can't be too many of these bores left among my readers. Their hectic schedules prevent them from devoting time to a phenomenon as improbable and untoward as a conversation between a child and an owl. They probably wouldn't have bought this novel at any rate.

The fact that an owl spoke to me in the woods of the Gaspé Peninsula surprised me less than the learned and pedantic tones he adopted. His accent and tone of voice reminded me of Pierre Elliott Trudeau. Sister Jeannette, Madame Nordet, and Japanese cartoons had prepared me for people walking on water, multiplying fishes, and panpipe-playing frogs, so I was able to take a nighttime encounter with a talking owl in my stride.

"Are you hurt, sir?"

"Not too badly. My foot hurts a little."

"You'll be fine. Are you lost, sir?"

"Yes, I think so."

"How amusing. If I perch on top of that birch tree over there, I can see the mice running around outside your house."

"So you know where I live."

"I know everything worth knowing within ten square kilometres. You do realize you are on my land?"

"Am I bothering you? I don't eat your field mice."

"That's not the point. I am a solitary being. Impatient and fiercely territorial."

"Yes, but we don't belong to the same species."

"You don't understand, young man. For me, there are two types of creature."

"What are they?"

"First, there is me. Then, there are the others."

"That's quite a simplistic way of looking at the world. I don't imagine it wins you many friends."

"I don't think you understand. An owl doesn't make *friends*. Anything that doesn't belong to my species is likely to become dinner."

"Even me? But how would you manage?"

"All I would have to do is gouge out your eyes and peck away at your head for long enough. You are well fed. You look tasty enough."

"But I don't understand. You never attack humans."

"Because there is still plenty of easier prey to catch. But make no mistake. The day I'm hungry enough, you're all going to get it. And you are on my land, after all."

"Yes, you said that already. *I* thought we were on *our* land. The king said so. This is our country. Before us, there were the Micmac, but they're all gone now. He never said anything about owls!"

"Hoo! Hoo! Listen to the little prince! Please inform His Majesty that this country belongs neither to you nor to the Micmac. Glooskap gave it to the great horned owl. You'll all leave soon enough!"

"I really do hope so, believe me. Do you know Jacques Brel?"

"Was he a Micmac?"

"No, he was Belgian. He always sang about leaving. You remind me of Jacques Brel. In "L'Ostendaise," for example, he sings: 'There are those who live and those who are at sea.'"

"Never heard that one. Is he still alive?"

"No, I think he's dead."

"—or at sea! Hoo! Hoo! Hoo! Ha! Ha! Ha! I'm the life and soul of the party this evening!"

"You're quite lighthearted for an animal that's supposed to symbolize wisdom."

"Since when has wisdom precluded lightheartedness, my dear boy? Besides, I have wings and I can fly, I'll have you know. I am no slave to gravity."

"I... I don't know. Sages are meant to be profound and..."

"Boring! They'd bore you to death, they would! Your species has never managed to be wise and lighthearted at once. That's their Achilles heel. They take themselves far too seriously."

"Great horned owl, please could you show me how to get home?"

"Yes, I dare say I could."

"Will you? I've lost the king and he's not the type to look back. He won't come back and get me."

"You seem to find that a shame. What does he owe you, this poor king?"

"Well, nothing really, apart from the fact that the whole trip was his idea."

"And you followed him?"

"Yes, I didn't have any choice."

"We always have a choice. That's what I tell my fledglings before I send them packing."

"You chase your fledglings from your territory?"

"Of course. You don't think I would leave, do you? I am a sedentary creature. When the rest of creation is one's larder, there is no need for one to keep moving around."

"You never move?"

"No. I hunt within a ten-kilometre radius. That's it. All of North America is divided into territories, each ruled by a great horned owl. No one treads on its talons. That was a promise from Glooskap."

"Glooskap promised you that?"

"Yes. Very clearly. He made this a land of sedentary creatures. We are the birds of the Gaspé Peninsula. We are born, we live, and we die in the very same place. What happens elsewhere is of no concern to us and is therefore of no importance whatsoever. Anyone who calls this into question is quite welcome to leave and look for answers elsewhere."

"I don't understand why Glooskap would have given you the right. He didn't ask for anything in return?"

"Oh, very little..."

"All the same. Nothing's free in this world. That's what Anne Boleyn always says."

"She's not wrong there."

"You're looking very thoughtful. What do you owe Glooskap in return?"

"The wind."

"The wind? You make the wind for him?"

"Yes, it's as simple as that. All the wind in North America is produced by the beating of our wings. Look! Just look at that wingspan! That's what I call a set of wings, my friend! Of course, we have to be careful. A long time ago, one great horned owl went a little overboard and got himself into a bit of bother. Since then, they've asked us to tone it down a little."

"I think I know the story. The Micmac broke one of his wings, right?"

"Indeed. Aren't you a bright young thing?"

"So you can make wind to order?"

"In theory, yes."

"And if one day, I don't know, someone should ask you to make a little more wind, enough to fly away on, enough to be carried far, far away, would you be able to?"

"Of course. Child's play. But who would ever want to leave here? What a strange idea!"

"I don't know, someone who wanted to go somewhere else. Someone who had had enough of it around here. Someone who is very unhappy here."

"That makes no sense at all! But I like the idea of flying someone away. Do you mean you? Would you like to leave now?"

"No, no! Not exactly. I'm not quite ready yet. We should agree on a signal for when the time comes."

"Why not? You live just there at the bottom of the field."

"Yes, but with the king, you never know when we might move."

"Move? Migrate you mean, like birds? That's a sign of weakness, you know. Leaving because the environment no longer suits you is a sign of weakness."

"It might be, but I don't have any choice there either."

"We always have a choice, I tell you. Now, let's *choose* the signal you will send me the day you would like to leave."

"A rocket?"

"No, it'll be gone in a flash. I have excellent eyesight, but I might miss it. And how would I know it came from you? Lots of people set off rockets for all kinds of reasons. The risk of misunderstanding is simply too great. I have a better idea. Why not poetry?"

"You want me to send you a poem as a signal?"

"Yes, a poem. Owls love poetry. When the time comes, recite a poem. There we go. Do it outside and make sure a chickadee can hear you. They can never keep anything to themselves. It will be so surprised, it will sing it all over the forest, *Chicka-deee-deee-deee-deee*. The white-throated sparrow will take up the song in its language, *Frederiiick, Frederiiick, Frederiiick*, then the wood thrush will strike up in its reedy, crystal clear tones. That's the part I'll hear. That will give you time to pack your bags and get ready to leave."

"That seems reasonable to me. And which poem should I recite?"

"Let's see now... Which ones do you know?"

"Mostly songs by Jacques Brel, which you don't seem to know. Maybe Nelligan's 'Vaisseau d'or'?"

"Too sad."

"'Le bateau ivre'? But I can't remember all of it by heart."

"Too long. There's no way the chickadee is going to translate all that!"

"Baudelaire's 'Albatross'?"

"Hmm, a bird. That's interesting. No, you shall recite 'Owls' by the very same Baudelaire. The message will be clear. It's my favourite poem. Truth be told, it's the only one I know by heart. I learned it because it's about me."

"I don't know that one. It's funny you don't know Brel, but you know 'Owls' by heart."

"For something to be of interest to me, it has to speak about me directly."

"That reminds me of a lot of people... But that means I'll have to learn the poem by heart!"

"Great! That way you'll have plenty of time to think before you leap. After all, leaving one's homeland is a serious undertaking. I'd never survive."

"You're a great horned owl. It's different."

"I must confess you have a point."

239

"But tell me, great horned owl, I'm willing to learn 'Owls' by heart, but how will the thrush know that the poem came from me and not someone else?"

"Have you lived here long?"

"Going on five years. Why?"

"How many times have you heard someone recite Baudelaire's 'Owls' over the past five years?"

"Fair enough."

"Believe me, if someone starts reciting Baudelaire around here, everyone will soon know about it. It can only be you. My dear friend, our plan is flawless. Rest assured that I will obey the moment I hear the signal, and you shall have your wind. No one can ever say I don't support the youth of today! Now, go find your king and make sure word of this conversation never crosses your lips."

"Thank you, great horned owl. May Glooskap protect you. Can you tell me how to get home?"

"It's very simple. I shall fly to the river and hoot to you from there. All you have to do is follow my hoot. From there, you will see the lights of your home."

"But you'll be right beside the river people. It's late; you might wake them."

"Do you really think they are asleep?"

"Yes, tomorrow is Monday. They have to get up early."

"How sweet! Right then, off I go. I shall guide you through the shadows. Farewell, young man! You will find 'Owls' in *Les fleurs du mal*. Good luck!"

The great horned owl kept his first promise. I found the king and my sister at the edge of the wood, walking hand in hand, forming a blurred silhouette against the tall grass.

Shortly after my encounter with the great horned owl, the court proclaimed Edict 4567, putting an end to the pastoral period of my childhood. Under the new edict, the entire court was to leave the territory by way of Route 4 to return to Matane. The king defended his decision by noting how close we would be to schools, businesses, and sources of entertainment. Boxes were packed, a change of address form was filled out for the Canada Post Corporation, and there was a new postal code to learn. The entire court moved into a red brick home by the side of a busy road in the small town. The king was right about entertainment being close at hand. The local paper was quick to give us all the proof we needed. One Wednesday, on page 8 of *La Voix gaspésienne*, the whole town was able to admire a photo of the uniformed king alongside a bubbly young lady none of us knew, visibly charmed by the king. Piqued, the queen brusquely retired to her quarters. The king began to come home very late. The palace doors began to slam again. The age of ice-cold stares, whispers, and yelling had returned. Everything fell back into place.

It was also at this time that my sister and I were sent to high school, a huge place with an enormous library where you could hide away and flee the movement and commotion of the ground floor. The pecking order at school in Saint-Ulric, while unpleasant, was at least clearly defined. The pecking order at the cavernous henhouse that was the high school in Matane was complex and fragmented. Various interest groups lived alongside each other in the huge school, each paying no heed to the other. Well-defined, watertight groups based on social class, postal code, and the price of their members' clothing formed, chose a clearly defined corner of the henhouse, and marked their territory. The school, in spite of its limitations, failings, and indescribable violence, had the advantage of having been designed by architects familiar with the pecking order. On days when the library was closed, you could hide under the stairs or at the end of deserted corridors to flee the deafening movement and commotion of the lockers and cafeteria. There, in the half-light, you could read in silence and block out, if only for a moment, the school's foul-smelling reality.

I had inflated expectations regarding my high school education. After the enormous void of elementary school, I had imagined my new school would be a place of reading, scintillating discussion, and unforgettable discoveries. I was quickly brought down to earth with a bump. First of all, I had three times as many teachers. To my horror, I quickly discovered that the school cherished math and science above all else. Teachers more like sorcerers than pedagogues taught biology, math, and physics. Math, in particular, was an especially serious form of worship you had better engage in if you hoped to have any sort of future. Languages and the humanities were about as useful as orchids, subjects for wandering, fickle minds. In my three years of high school there, I was given two novels to read. The first, *Of Mice and Men* by John Steinbeck was handed out in October; we were to read it by November 15. Trembling with happiness, I twice devoured the sad tale of Lennie, the simpleton overly fond of soft things. The queen was a big help. It turned out she knew exactly which questions to ask about the novel. She quizzed me on George's responsibility toward his companion in misfortune. "Was he right to kill Lennie out of love?" I didn't know. I could feel something else in the air, but it wasn't me or my boring chemistry classes that were going to be done away with out of love. She even suggested I read other books by the same author, a big favourite of hers. I read *East of Eden* over her shoulder, and was shaken to the core.

And so I feverishly prepared my observations on *Of Mice and Men* for November 15. Convinced that my time to shine had come, I even went so far as to link the author's moral dilemma to the story of Cain and Abel, as Anne Boleyn had suggested. I felt ready to answer any question, however obscure and convoluted. The day came. I consulted my reading notes one last time before the class that was going to make my name as a student. The class began with tedious grammar exercises, followed by a dictation. There were only five minutes left when the teacher suddenly glanced down at a note he had scribbled to himself on a scrap of paper. He had clearly forgotten something. "Oh yes! The book!" he exclaimed. There were only four minutes left. We would have to be brief. "What did you think of it?" he inquired, looking at his watch. I had expected every question bar that one. What had I thought of it? He wanted a two-minute answer? Right now? In front of everybody? "No one wants to answer? So was it good or not?" I had never imagined it was possible to treat literature like a brand of canned soup. A girl ventured a response. "I haven't finished it. I didn't understand everything that happened." The teacher looked indifferent, glanced at the back of the book, pulled an uncertain face, and said, "Well, I think that says it all." Then the bell rang. We never spoke about *Of Mice and Men*, or any other book, in French class again. Although we often talked about the film classes our teacher had taken years ago at Laval University in Quebec City. The experience seemed to have left a lasting impression on him. I concluded that literature was impenetrable, that at the end of the day all it was good for was calling out to the animal gods in the forests of Canada and that its only purpose was to bring about sudden, windy change when all else failed. Clearly, I wasn't there yet. Literature was to once again become an unspoiled continent that I would continue to explore alone, armed with a machete and a rifle, discovering behind each moss-covered rock whole worlds whose only purpose was to change mine, little by little. I never found out what "Of Mice and Men" meant. I still read it today, wondering if it is possible to kill someone or something out of love.

After this brief literary episode, the waltz of equations and Cartesian diagrams started up again, more vigorously than ever. Physics was added to the biol-ogy-chemistry-math cocktail. At age fifteen, the world of my education could be summed up as a terrifying egg-shaped quadratic curve, dropping down through my exercise books like a nuclear warhead.

Events moved fast at the royal palace. The incident of the photograph in *La Voix gaspésienne* took on worrying and unexpected proportions. The lady who had brought scandal upon the court was called Jane Seymour, a notori-ous courtesan from Matane who had set her sights on becoming queen. Aside from the political and sentimental intrigue, the reasons behind such a move were not alto-gether in Jane Seymour's favour. She was childless, worked off and on in some office or other, and her only attribute was a finely honed appreciation for fashion and acces-sories. While Anne Boleyn was an expert when it came to compound interest and making money, Jane Seymour knew nothing of mathematics—but she sure knew how to spend. The contrast between the new pretender to the throne and the incumbent surprised outsiders, but those close to Henry VIII barely batted an eyelid.

And so the king charged an internal commission with coming up with grounds for separation. He needed something that would be deemed acceptable by the public. All spoke up against deposing the queen. No edict provided for her replacement. No one had ever imagined that her powers might be suspended, let alone that she might be deposed or sent into exile. The king called on the advisers who had helped him get rid of

Catherine of Aragon round about the time of the 1976 Olympic Games. These conscientious and scrupulous advisers nevertheless had to admit they could provide the king with no counsel on the matter. They could undo an unhappy marriage and legitimize a divorce in the eyes of the people, but since Anne Boleyn and Henry VIII had never been married, their expertise was of no use. "We cannot annul what does not exist," they declared, before throwing in the towel. Replying to Henry VIII in this tone was not without risk. Once they had finished, the king sentenced them all to death and set up a new council tasked with coming up with convincing arguments for the commission that would allow and legitimize the deposition of Anne Boleyn and the coronation of Jane Seymour. The former advisers were decapitated by a celebrated executioner, the same one who had executed the clergy responsible for the king's unhappy childhood. The ceremony had a galvanizing effect on the new advisers appointed by the king against their will to help get him out of this matrimonial impasse.

Anne Boleyn's Deposition Committee, created and named in 1984, bore the weighty responsibility of substituting one queen for another without weakening the king's power. The political hullabaloo caused by Catherine of Aragon's deposition in 1977 was still fresh in the mind. This time round, the king's power had been whittled away to the point where the commission now feared that a premature and poorly planned ousting in the Anne Boleyn affair might prove fatal to the throne.

The fate reserved for the first advisers preoccupied the members of the new committee, who feared the worst in the event of failure.

The queen was first reproached for her stranglehold on the kingdom's purse strings. The king demanded greater spending power. But the argument was shaky, and the queen quickly quashed it. "I wasn't the one who spent all our savings building a boat that isn't even finished yet!" she told the fourth committee hearing.

And so they changed tack. The king's advisers brought up the recurrent conflicts between the queen and Catherine of Aragon's children, who appeared to still feel dogged resentment toward the queen. As though to support this theory, my sister chose that very summer to pull off a coup that would help the king move ahead with his projects. It just so happened that Micheline Raymond, professional cook and the first queen, invited her daughter to become a kitchen hand for the summer in the restaurant where she worked. My sister took her up on the invitation, thereby upsetting the delicate balance of the kingdom and confirming that Catherine of Aragon, despite the censure surrounding her name, had only to pick up the phone to bring the children that destiny had plucked away from her running back to the family fold. The Deposition Committee flogged this horse for all they were worth. Anne Boleyn, as though to defend herself from these attacks on her personality and her general inflexibility and impatience, became more accommodating and less distant.

It goes without saying that the reasons invoked by the committee fell short. The queen could perhaps be deposed for some reason or another, but it would be difficult, if not nigh on impossible, to get the kingdom to accept the coronation of Jane Seymour, whose dubious reputation raised fears of a reign blighted by instability and recklessness. That was to underestimate Henry VIII's determination to install by his side the woman who came to simper at the palace gates with a little more insistence each day. A flurry of edicts added to the Deposition Committee's interminable deliberations, some of which rescinded the edicts of summer 1977, notably Edict 101. We were once again allowed to talk about Micheline Raymond, professional cook, within the palace walls, even in the presence of the little brother, who discovered, at the age of seven, that we were half-brothers and became aware of Catherine of Aragon's existence for the first time.

Tensions at the palace didn't stop me continuing to plan my escape. The prospect of Jane Seymour's ascension to the throne simply accelerated the process. At fifteen, I already knew better than the poor, desperate kid who, one forlorn evening, had thought he might hop aboard a ship bound for Murmansk. What I had lost in naïveté, I had gained in determination. At school I would sometimes hang around the guidance counsellor's office in between two math exercises. The role of a guidance counsellor, like that of a Silva compass, is to help you find your way. Ours was a very nice man with a moustache, who always wore the same grey wool jacket and whose job was to test students eager to set career goals for themselves as early as possible in their adolescence.

One of these tests involved answering one hundred multiple choice questions on a computer, which then came up with a profession based on your responses. Some students left the office satisfied that the computer had spat out "doctor," "gamekeeper," or "banker." Others, having supplied the wrong answers, were condemned to become "grocery baggers" or "crane operators." Curiously, no one ever got "guidance counsellor." In my case, the computer hesitated a second. I silently hoped for "pope" or "member of parliament" and was sure I had given the right answers to provide just such a result. The paper came out of the printer. "Actuary." "What does an actuary do?" I asked my dear guidance counsellor. "Lots of math." The oracles can be cruel.

While my guidance counsellor settled another student's future, my eyes fell on a recessed shelf, hidden in a corner and lightly covered in dust. "What're those?" I asked. "Those? They're programs for abroad or for English-speaking Canada. Be careful: they're dusty." I picked up a few booklets at random and stuffed them into my bag. Back at the royal palace, the queen approved of the computer's decision to make an actuary out of me. The test, she explained, was based on the answers given by an extensive number of actuaries, doctors, crane operators, gamekeepers, and so on. Seventy-four percent of my answers matched those provided by actuaries. The people who had designed the test hadn't been able to quiz a large number of popes, so that profession wasn't one of the possibilities. I felt slightly relieved. "Actuaries earn a lot of money," she murmured thoughtfully. I was more concerned with finding out if they travelled.

But the atmosphere at the palace wasn't conducive to career studies. The king was still waiting for Anne Boleyn's Deposition Committee to submit its report to the commission. The unfortunate committee members had exhausted all arguments, and the sovereign's patience was wearing thin. Barring a sudden stroke of inspiration, their days were numbered. To dispel all doubt as to his intentions, one evening the king sent a randomly chosen adviser to the Tower to be decapitated. The scene jolted the survivors into action, and they redoubled their efforts to satisfy the sovereign. Although he was used to thinking everything through for himself, the king left this job up to his advisers, keen to give the impression that the decision did not come from him but from an outside body, making him look touchingly vulnerable. Once again he was right. One evening when it seemed all was lost, just as the committee chair was steeling himself to swallow two cyanide pills, someone stood up and shouted "Eureka!" It was a bold solution. Since the queen herself had brought up the boat argument to fend off accusations of avarice, the committee proposed using the boat project as the central argument in the deposing of Anne Boleyn. The entire court was summoned for an extraordinary session in the Sapphire Room. The king, visibly satisfied with the findings, allowed the report to be submitted to the commission. The argument went as follows. The queen's unkind comments about the king, especially his project to build a boat, had greatly pained His Majesty. The queen was well aware of the importance the king placed on this as-yet-unfinished project. Her comment had cast doubt on the possibility of the king ever finishing his project and jeopardized its completion. Through her lack of faith, she had belittled Henry VIII's aspirations and relegated his lifelong dream to the ranks of mere fantasy. The committee could not allow the queen to cast aspersions on such an important matter. One adviser went as far as to suggest that the queen's doubts surrounding the project could easily descend into opposition, something the court could not tolerate. Finally, they argued that the danger was too great and that the queen's doubts amounted to high treason, punishable by death. It was decided, therefore, that the queen be put to death before sunset.

A heavy silence fell over the Sapphire Room. The committee members stared at the floor, unable to bear the looks of disapproval that their daring proposal would surely draw. From the back of the room, a Carmelite nun who had been acting as a silent, neutral observer stood up. To signal her intention to speak, she cleared her throat and put down the rosary beads she had been clutching throughout the deliberations. She looked like a much younger Sister Jeannette. She had the same voice and the same intelligent look. The petite woman was not intimidated by the advisers' furious looks. She began to speak. "Your Royal Highnesses, members of the royal family, honourable committee members, esteemed advisers, and respectful subjects, please allow me to say that the Church deplores the fact that the committee has failed to consider the little brother's well-being before arriving at this decision. I insist that my voice be heard today for the first time in thirty years and that my words be remembered." The king smiled as he listened to the poor Carmelite. He looked almost moved. He took a moment to remind all present that since the edicts of 1977, members of the clergy had lost the right to speak on any matter whatsoever and thanked the nun for her intervention. Upon his signal, two guards seized the Carmelite by the arms and led her to the Tower, where she was executed in silence. She offered no resistance. The sad opera resumed in the Sapphire Room.

The king and Jane Seymour appeared satisfied with the judicial ruling. Flabbergasted by the committee's audacity, the queen stood up and crossed the room, holding her son by the hand. Before passing through the door, she turned, looked at each person in turn, and slowly removed her crown. "I do declare, Sire, that I am not so attached to it. If it has been decided that the queen be decapitated before sunset, then so be it," she said, placing the crown on Jane Seymour's head.

Jane Seymour smiled foolishly, not realizing that Anne Boleyn had just crowned her queen and thereby condemned her to death. Anne Boleyn and her son left the castle with their heads held high, with the wide-eyed committee looking on. I watched with interest, thinking of the great horned owl, who had maintained that we always have a choice. Anne Boleyn, the kingdom's despotic sovereign, taught us that day that it was possible to live in a monarchy without demeaning oneself. The deposed queen slammed the door on her way out as only she knew how. It was the finest of her entire career. All doors slammed in the future would be measured against that one.

Jane Seymour applauded proudly as she looked at the vexed king. She asked childishly, "You know your boat? Can it go all the way to Florida?"

Thanks to the king's deft political machinations, Jane Seymour was still alive the day after her coronation. The king had vetoed the committee's ruling, and all its members were decapitated the same day before the executioner could complain about having come all that way for nothing. The subjects had their spectacle, Jane Seymour was crowned, and the royal couple could finally show their love for one another in public. It is worth noting that the king's veto had not existed until then. He had had his advisers vote in favour of it at the double, just before he had them executed. The veto could be used retroactively on all decisions, no matter when they had been made or who had made them.

No one would want a king whose powers were limited by previous commitments. Anne Boleyn was never mentioned in the court again. Edict 101, which banned uttering the name of Micheline Raymond, professional cook, was amended to include Anne Boleyn. In the palace of Henry VIII, life became one long succession of opening and closing doors. A series of short, sharp bangs that caused no end of drafts. The age of reason and Cartesian thinking was over. The period that followed was marked by profound questioning that the new queen didn't shy away from.

"What's your sign?"

"Gemini."

"I'm Aquarius. Those two signs always get on well together! That's just great!"

While I had spent the previous regime having to work out the most fiendish equations, solve devilishly difficult Rubik's cubes, and translate spy novels in order to curry favour with the crown, henceforth I would have only to read the horoscope page. In the short term, the reign of Jane Seymour brought with it some interesting changes for me and my sister. Naturally, we moved to another house. Then, we saw less and less of the king. In fact, we hardly saw him at all. I thought back to the beached whale in Matane in the summer of 1977 and the message I had read in its entrails. It seemed to me that the Kingdom our Father had promised us was taking its sweet time coming. For this ersatz family that had managed to struggle on for years, barely keeping a grip on real life, the end came well before the king's boat ever hit the water. At the time, people spoke of separated families, reconstituted families, and dysfunctional families; mine had been pulverized. My sister ended up leaving the castle. I remained at home, alone with the forms I had taken from the guidance counsellor's office.

Which country would you like to visit?

My thoughts turned to Heidi in the Alps. She would have to go back there one day.

I borrowed *Les fleurs du mal* from the library.

As we listened to the committee hand down its verdict, I remember how Anne Boleyn had stared into the distance, into a black abyss into which spiralled figures and equations. For his part, Henry VIII hungrily scanned the horizon for women and beer. Sometimes you hesitate between two visions of the future. Neither direction appealed to me. I decided to blaze my own path across this wasteland, spurred on by memories of the laughter of Micheline Raymond, professional cook, and a poem by Baudelaire.

I learned the two quatrains and two tercets in no time. I waited for a cloudless night before I left. In the port of Matane, right beside a nervous chickadee, I sent my message to the great horned owl.

*Owls*

*Under the dark yews which shade them,*
*The owls are perched in rows,*

*Like so many strange gods,*
*Darting their red eyes. They meditate.*

*Without budging they will remain*
*Till that melancholy hour*
*When, pushing back the slanting sun,*
*Darkness will take up its abode.*

*Their attitude teaches the wise*
*That in this world one must fear*
*Movement and commotion;*

*Man, enraptured by a passing shadow,*
*Forever bears the punishment*
*Of having tried to change his place.*

The black-capped chickadee was taken aback for an instant, then, slightly perplexed, perched on a lilac and struck up a long *chick-a-deee-deee-deee-deee-deee*, repeated several times over, until a passing white-throated sparrow picked up the signal in the distance and translated it into its own language, high above the treetops on the Gaspé Peninsula. *Frederiiick, Frederiiick, Frederiiick! Frederiiick, Frederiiick, Frederiiick!* The night resounded with its cries for a good hour. I waited in the red sunset. Far away on the other side of the St. Lawrence, the lights of Baie-Comeau were already glistening. Then the wood thrush—the soprano of our forests—struck up the loveliest song of all: *karlakar-*

*lak tirloo treeeee!* I could make out the deft wisdom of Baudelaire's poetry in its complex melody. The sun descended over the North Shore. I heard the sinister hoot of the great horned owl. My signal had reached him. The wind picked up, swept under my shirt, rushed through my hair, and forced me to close my eyes. On the wharf in the port of Matane, right where sad little Laika still runs around on winter nights, I held out my arms. Then, as light as Nadia Comaneci flying between two uneven bars, I let go of the upper bar forever to sketch a long curve eastward across the night sky. On the ground, on the huge green mat of the Gaspé Peninsula, I could make out my little henhouse, chickens by the thousand, winkles, a giant fibreglass shrimp, the skeleton of a beached whale and, in the distance, a huge owl frantically beating its wings atop a tall fir tree. The song of the black-capped chickadee, the white-throated sparrow, the wood thrush, and the great horned owl—the soundtrack to my country—was the last thing I remembered, the most beautiful, the most precious of all. The only thing I decided to bring with me, along with the memory of the laughter of Micheline Raymond, professional cook. Because at the end of the day, that's really all we're left with: just a name, the sound of a bird singing, a laugh, the punishment of having tried to change one's place.

# The Canary (1986)

Austria, September 22, 1986

My dear sister,

*Grüßgott*! I hope my letter finds you well. It was a long journey. I discovered a very strange phenomenon on the plane on the way over. You won't believe me, but as soon as you sit down on a plane, you stop feeling those little earthquakes. I highly recommend it!

I'm a little worried by your letters. So the king and Jane Seymour are already at daggers drawn? And who is this Anne of Cleves you speak of? Our new queen? You know, here in Austria they got rid of the monarchy over sixty years ago. I think they had the right idea.

I've come to quite a strange place. First off, I'm living in a tiny village (the one you can see at the foot of the mountain on the postcard) beside a lake. The landscape is straight out of *Heidi*. People bring their dogs with them absolutely everywhere, even to restaurants. Fortunately, there's no dog where I'm staying. Frau S. has a caged canary in the kitchen called Hans. On Saturday afternoon, the radio always plays the same Mozart piece before the news. As soon as the music begins, the bird begins to chirp away in its cage. He recognizes the music and wants to sing along. It's almost as though he's trying to imitate it—or showing how happy he is to hear it. I'm not sure which. *"Hansi, du Depp!"* Frau S. shouts at him. "Hansi, you idiot!" It's strange. She almost always wears black. I asked her one day why she wears so much *schwartz*. I thought she might be mourning someone. But that wasn't it at all! She wears black because she likes the colour. *"Weil ich eine Hexe bin!"* she joked. Ha! A witch indeed! Speaking of Frau S., I think it's time I told you a little more about the people who live here.

There are four of them. The father, mother, and two sons, Markus and Christian. One of the boys is my age and goes to the same school. The other is about the same age as our little brother. Speaking of whom, have you seen him recently? The Austrians have some strange habits. When I arrived, the father wanted to put my things away into a closet for me. As if I couldn't do it by myself. But that's not all. The two boys don't lift a finger.

I still have yet to see them do the dishes. They wouldn't so much as water a plant. They stare at me in amazement every time I try to help out around the house. It's not as if I enjoy it; I just can't help myself. I tidy things away and do some cleaning. The mother looks at me as though I'm mad.

Meals are stranger still. We all eat together at the same time every evening. And hold on to your hat: Last night, Herr S. got out a bottle of wine. I kept waiting for him to fall under the table after an hour or two. But no! They finished their bottle and laughed until it was time for the news. I have no idea what they were laughing at; I only understand the most basic sentences. I haven't said much since I got here. They watch the news every night at 7:30. That usually makes them sad, but not for long. They'll often go on drinking while they watch the news, but even then there are no shouting matches. I'm beginning to wonder what kind of house I'm in. It's all very strange. I'll keep you posted.

You should also know that I've lost the little cod scales I used to have behind my knees. I woke up one morning and there they were on the sheets, shining like little diamonds. I've put them in the envelope. Would you be kind enough to throw them into the St. Lawrence for me? I think that's the best place for them.

I'm very sorry about the king's boat. I would never have thought the hull would end up at the scrapyard. What a waste! You know, I read somewhere that even Jacques Brel got rid of his boat, so...

261

I've got to go finish my homework now. My Austrian teachers give us plenty to read. Tonight it's Shakespeare's *Taming of the Shrew*. Herr and Frau S. say they'll take me to see the play in Vienna this winter. Any news of Anne Boleyn?

Your little brother

P. S. I swear my nose is always buried in the dictionary. Today, I learned that "in vain" translates as *vergeblich*. It's a funny language, isn't it?

QC Fiction brings you the very best of a new generation of Quebec
storytellers, sharing surprising, interesting novels
in flawless English translation.


Coming soon from QC Fiction:


*BROTHERS* by David Clerson
*THE UNKNOWN HUNTSMAN* by Jean-Michel Fortier
*EXTRATERRESTRIAL BODIES* by Pierre-Luc Landry

Visit **qcfiction.com** for details and to subscribe
to a full season of QC Fiction titles.

RECYCLED
Paper made from
recycled material
FSC® C100212
FSC
www.fsc.org

Printed in May 2016
by Gauvin Press,
Gatineau, Québec